Agatha

Agatha Christie (1890-1976) is known throughout the world as the Queen of Crime. Her books have sold over a billion copies in English with another billion in over 100 foreign languages. She is the most widely published and translated author of all time and in any language; only the Bible and Shakespeare have sold more copies. She is the author of 80 crime novels and short story collections, 19 plays, and six other novels. *The Mousetrap*, her most famous play, was first staged in 1952 in London and is still performed there – it is the longest-running play in history.

Agatha Christie's first novel was published in 1920. It featured Hercule Poirot, the Belgian detective who has become the most popular detective in crime fiction since Sherlock Holmes. Collins has published Agatha Christie since 1926.

This series has been especially created for readers worldwide whose first language is not English. Each story has been shortened, and the vocabulary and grammar simplified to make it accessible to readers with a good intermediate knowledge of the language.

The following features are included after the story:

A **List of characters** to help the reader identify who is who, and how they are connected to each other. **Cultural notes** to explain historical and other references. A **Glossary** of words that some readers may not be familiar with are explained. There is also a **Recording** of the story.

CALGARY PUBLIC LIBRARY

NOV / / 2017

CALGARY PUBLIC LIBRARY

NOV 1 1 2012

Agatha Christie

The Murder of Roger Ackroyd

Collins

HarperCollins Publishers
The News Building
1 London Bridge Street
London
SE1 9GF

Collins ® is a registered trademark of HarperCollins Publishers Limited.

This *Collins English Readers Edition* published 2012

Reprint 10 9 8 7 6 5 4 3 2

Original text first published in Great Britain by Collins 1926

AGATHA CHRISTIE™ POIROT™ The Murder of Roger Ackroyd™
Copyright © 1926 Agatha Christie Limited. All rights reserved.
Copyright © 2012 The Murder of Roger Ackroyd™ abridged edition
Agatha Christie Limited. All rights reserved.
www.agathachristie.com

ISBN: 978-0-00-745156-2

A catalogue record for this book is available from the British Library.

Educational Consultant: Fitch O'Connell

Cover by crushed.co.uk © HarperCollins/Agatha Christie Ltd 2008

Typeset by Aptara in India

Printed and bound in Great Britain

All rights reserved. No part of this publication may be reproduced,
stored in a retrieval system, or transmitted, in any form or by any means,
electronic, mechanical, photocopying, recording or otherwise, without
the prior permission of the publishers.

This book is sold subject to the condition that it shall not, by way of trade
or otherwise, be lent, re-sold, hired out or otherwise circulated without
the publisher's prior consent in any form of binding or cover other than
that in which it is published and without a similar condition including this
condition being imposed on the subsequent purchaser.

HarperCollins does not warrant that www.collinselt.com or any other
website mentioned in this title will be provided uninterrupted, that
any website will be error free, that defects will be corrected, or that the
website or the server that makes it available are free of viruses or bugs.
For full terms and conditions please refer to the site terms provided on
the website.

Contents

Chapter 1 Dr Sheppard At The Breakfast Table

Mrs Ferrars died on the night of the 16th September – a Thursday. I was sent for at eight o'clock on Friday morning and a few minutes after nine I reached home again.

'Is that you, James?' my sister Caroline called. 'Come and get your breakfast!'

I walked into the dining-room.

'You've had an early call.'

'Yes,' I said. 'King's Paddock. Mrs Ferrars.'

'I know. Annie told me.'

Annie is our maid.

'Well?' my sister demanded.

'A sad business. She must have died in her sleep.'

'I know,' said my sister again.

'I didn't know myself until I got there! If Annie knows . . .'

'It was the <u>milkman</u> who told me. The Ferrars' <u>cook</u> told him. What did she die of?'

'She died of an overdose of <u>veronal</u>. She's been taking it for sleeplessness. She must have taken too much.'

'No,' said Caroline. 'She took it on purpose! I told you she poisoned her husband. And ever since she's been <u>haunted</u> by what she did.'

I told Caroline that her whole idea was nonsense.

'Nonsense?' said Caroline. 'I'm sure she's left a letter <u>confessing</u> everything.'

'She didn't leave a letter,' I said sharply.

'Oh!' said Caroline. 'So you *did* inquire about that, did you?'

Chapter 2 Who's Who in King's Abbot

There are only two houses of any importance in King's Abbot. One is King's Paddock, left to Mrs Ferrars by her husband. The other, Fernly Park, is owned by Roger Ackroyd, an extremely successful businessman of nearly fifty years of age. He gives generously to village activities, though he is said to be extremely <u>mean</u> in personal spending. When he was just twenty-one, Ackroyd married a beautiful <u>widow</u>, Mrs Paton, who had one child, Ralph. Sadly, Mrs Ackroyd was an <u>alcoholic</u> and drank herself to death. Ralph, now twenty-five, has been a continual <u>source</u> of trouble to Ackroyd. However, we are all very <u>fond</u> of Ralph in King's Abbot.

After her husband's death, Ackroyd and Mrs Ferrars were always seen together, and it was thought that at the end of a period of <u>mourning</u>, Mrs Ferrars would become Mrs Roger Ackroyd.

The Ferrarses only came to live here just over a year ago. Before that, the whole village had confidently expected Ackroyd to marry his housekeeper, Miss Russell. At the same time, his widowed sister-in-law, Mrs Cecil Ackroyd, with her daughter, came to stay with Ackroyd – and she certainly disapproved of him marrying his housekeeper.

I went on my <u>round</u>, my thoughts returning to Mrs Ferrars' death. I had last seen her only yesterday, walking with Ralph Paton. I had been very surprised to see him. He and his stepfather had argued very badly six months ago and he hadn't been seen in King's Abbot since. I was still thinking of it when I came face to face with Roger Ackroyd himself.

'Sheppard!' he exclaimed. 'This is a terrible business! I've got to talk to you. Can you come back with me now?'

'No. I've got patients to visit still, and <u>surgery</u>.'

'Then come for dinner tonight. At 7.30. I – Damn! Here's old Miss Gannett coming. I don't want to have to talk to her. See you tonight, Sheppard.'

Miss Gannett was full of <u>gossip</u>. Wasn't it sad about poor dear Mrs Ferrars? People were saying she had been a <u>drug addict</u>.

I went home, thoughtful, to find several patients waiting for me to begin surgery.

Chapter 3 The Man Who Grew
Vegetable Marrows

I told Caroline at lunch that I would be dining at Fernly.

'Excellent,' she said. 'You'll hear all about it. By the way, why is Ralph staying at the _Three Boars_ pub? He arrived yesterday morning. And last night he went out to meet a girl. I don't know who she is.'

It must have been very hard for Caroline to have to admit that she didn't know.

'But I can guess,' continued my sister. 'His "cousin", Flora Ackroyd is, of course, no relation really to Ralph Paton. They are secretly <u>engaged</u>. Ackroyd disapproves and they have to meet secretly.'

I began to talk about our new neighbour, which stopped Caroline saying more about her romantic theory. The house next door, The Larches, has recently been rented by a stranger. To Caroline's annoyance, she has not been able to find out anything about him, except that his name is Mr Porrott, he is a foreigner, and he is interested in growing vegetable marrows. That is not the sort of information Caroline wants. She wants to know where he comes from, what he does, whether he is married – and so on.

'My dear Caroline,' I said. 'There's no doubt that the man is a <u>retired</u> hairdresser. Look at that moustache of his.'

I escaped into the garden. I was digging up <u>weeds</u> when a heavy object flew past my ears and fell at my feet. It was a marrow! Over the wall there appeared an egg-shaped head, partly covered with suspiciously black hair, a huge moustache, and a pair of green eyes. It was the mysterious Mr Porrott.

'A thousand pardons, <u>Monsieur</u>. For some months now I grow the marrows. This morning I become angry with them. I seize one. I throw him over the wall. Monsieur, I am ashamed. Do not worry. It is not a habit with me. But Monsieur, do you not think that a man may work to reach a peaceful retirement, and then find that, after all, he wants the old busy days back, and the occupation that he thought he was so glad to leave?'

'Yes,' I said, thinking how strangely he spoke English. 'I know that feeling well. I have always wanted to travel, to see the world. A year ago I <u>inherited</u> some money – enough to allow me to realize a dream, yet I am still here.'

My little neighbour nodded. 'Habits are very hard to break. And Monsieur, my work was the most interesting work there is in the world; the study of human nature!'

Clearly a retired hairdresser. Who knows the secrets of human nature better than a hairdresser?

'Also, I had a friend who for many years never left my side. Occasionally he behaved stupidly enough to make me afraid, but his honest opinions, the pleasure of delighting and surprising him by my greater intelligence – I miss these things more than I can tell you.'

'He died?'

'Not so. He lives now in the Argentine.'

'In the Argentine,' I said, jealously.

Mr Porrott looked at me sympathetically.

'You will go there, yes?' he asked.

I shook my head with a <u>sigh</u>. 'I could have gone a year ago. But I was <u>foolish</u> and <u>speculated</u>.'

'Not those new oilfields?' he asked.

'I thought about them, but in the end I chose a gold mine in Western Australia.'

My neighbour was regarding me with a strange expression.

'It is <u>Fate</u>, that I should live next to a man who would seriously consider investing in oilfields, and gold mines. And you are a doctor, a man who knows the stupidity of most things. Well, well, we are neighbours. Please, you must give your excellent sister my best marrow.'

He bent down, picked up a huge marrow and gave it to me.

'Indeed,' said the little man cheerfully, 'this has not been a wasted morning. I have met a man who in some ways resembles my old friend. By the way, you must know everyone in this village. Who is the young man with the very dark hair and eyes, and the handsome face?'

'Captain Ralph Paton,' I said. 'He is the <u>stepson</u> of Mr Ackroyd of Fernly Park.'

'I should have guessed. Mr Ackroyd spoke of him many times.'

'You know Mr Ackroyd?' I asked, surprised.

'Mr Ackroyd knew me in London – when I worked there. I have asked him to say nothing of my profession down here. I have not even tried to correct the way the local people pronounce my name. So, Captain Ralph Paton, and he is engaged to the beautiful Miss Flora.'

'Who told you so?'

'Mr Ackroyd. He put some pressure on the young man. That is never wise. A young man should marry to please himself – not to please a stepfather, even though he expects to inherit a great deal of money from him.'

I was confused. I could not imagine Ackroyd discussing the marriage with a hairdresser.

At that moment my sister called me from the house. I went in. Caroline had just come back from the village. She began talking immediately. 'I met Mr Ackroyd and I asked him about Ralph.

He was <u>astonished</u>. He had no idea the boy was down here. Then he went on to tell me that Ralph and Flora are engaged. And I told him that Ralph was staying at the *Three Boars*.'

'Caroline,' I said, 'do you never think that you might do harm by repeating everything you hear?'

'Nonsense! People should know things. I think Mr Ackroyd went straight to the *Three Boars*, but if so he didn't find Ralph there, because as I was coming through the <u>woods</u> . . .'

'Coming through the woods?' I interrupted.

'It was such a lovely day. The autumn colours are so perfect at this time of year.'

Caroline does not like woods at any time of year. But our local woods are the only place where you can talk with a young woman unseen by the whole village.

'Anyway, I heard voices. One was Ralph Paton's. The other was a girl's. She said something I didn't hear and Ralph answered very angrily. "My dear girl," he said, "the old man will <u>disinherit</u> me, which means I'll be very, very poor! If he doesn't, I will be a very, very rich man when he dies, so I don't want him to change his <u>will</u>. You leave it to me, and don't worry." Unfortunately, just then I stepped on a piece of wood which broke and made a noise, and they moved away. So I wasn't able to see who the girl was. Who could it have been?'

I made an excuse about a patient and went out, but I went straight to the *Three Boars*. Ralph had not inherited his mother's addiction to alcohol, but he *was* <u>self-indulgent</u> and <u>extravagant</u>. Nevertheless, his friends were all <u>devoted</u> to him. At the *Three Boars* I was told that Captain Paton had just come in. I went up to his room.

'Why, it's Sheppard! The one person I am glad to see in this place. Have a drink, won't you?'

'Thanks,' I said, 'I will.'

He pressed the bell, then sat down with a sigh. 'I'm in a complete mess; I just don't know what to do next. It's my stepfather.'

'What has he done?'

'It isn't what he's done, but what he's likely to do.'

'If I could help —' I suggested.

He shook his head. 'It's good of you, Doctor. But I've got to do this on my own . . .'

Chapter 4 Dinner at Fernly

As Parker, the Fernly Park butler, took my coat, Ackroyd's secretary, a pleasant young man called Geoffrey Raymond, passed through the hall on his way to Ackroyd's study, with his hands full of business documents.

'Good evening, Doctor. Coming to dine? Or is this a professional call?'

This referred to my black bag, which I had put down on the oak table. I explained that I expected to be called to deliver a baby at any moment. Raymond went on his way, saying,

'Go into the drawing room. I'll tell Mr Ackroyd you're here.'

I noticed, just as I was turning the handle of the drawing-room door, a sound from inside – like the shutting down of a sash window. As I walked in, Miss Russell, Ackroyd's housekeeper, was just coming out. What a good-looking woman she was!

'I'm afraid I'm early,' I said.

'Oh! I don't think so. It's gone half-past seven, Dr Sheppard. But I must be going. I only came in to see if the flowers were all right.'

She went, and I saw, of course, what I had forgotten – that the windows were long French ones opening on the terrace. So that could not have been the sound I heard.

I noticed the silver table, which displays silver and other valuable items. Its glass top lifts, and inside, as I knew from other visits, were one or two pieces of old silver, a baby shoe which had belonged to King Charles I, and a number of African pieces. Wanting to examine one of the figures more closely, I lifted the lid. It slipped through my fingers and fell. The sound I had heard was this lid being shut down!

I was still bending over the silver table when Flora Ackroyd came in. Nobody can help admiring her. She has pale gold hair, her eyes are the deepest blue, and her skin is the colour of cream and roses.

'Congratulate me, Dr Sheppard,' said Flora. She held out her left hand. On the third finger was a beautiful single <u>pearl</u> ring. 'I'm going to marry Ralph. Uncle is very pleased.'

I took both her hands in mine.

'My dear,' I said, 'I hope you'll be very happy.'

'We've been engaged for about a month,' continued Flora, 'but it was only announced yesterday. Uncle is going to do up Cross-stones, and give it to us to live in, and we're going to pretend to farm. Really, we shall hunt all the winter and go to London for the season.'

Just then the widowed Mrs Cecil Ackroyd came in. I am sorry to say I cannot stand Mrs Ackroyd. She is all teeth and bones, with small pale blue eyes, and however friendly her words may be, her eyes always remain coldly calculating. Had I heard about Flora's engagement, she wondered.

Mrs Ackroyd was interrupted as the drawing-room door opened once more.

'You know Major Blunt, don't you, Doctor?'

'Yes, indeed.'

Hector Blunt has shot more wild animals in Africa and India than any man living and every two years he spends a fortnight at Fernly. A man of medium height and well-built, Blunt's face is deeply suntanned, and strangely expressionless. He is not a man who talks a lot!

He said now, 'How are you, Sheppard?' and then stood in front of the <u>fireplace</u> looking over our heads as though he saw something very interesting happening in the far distance.

'Major Blunt,' said Flora, 'Could you tell me about these African things? I'm sure you know what they all are.'

Blunt joined Flora at the silver table and they bent over it together.

★ ★ ★

Dinner was not a cheerful affair. Ackroyd ate almost nothing and immediately after dinner he took me to his study.

'Once we've had coffee, we won't be disturbed again,' he explained. 'I told Raymond to make sure we won't be interrupted.'

As Parker entered with the coffee tray, Ackroyd sat down in an armchair in front of the fire.

'That pain I was getting after eating – it's back again,' he said. 'You must give me some more of those tablets.'

I realized that he wanted to pretend to Parker that our discussion was a medical one. I cooperated. 'I brought some with me. They're in my bag in the hall so I'll go and get them.'

'Don't go yourself. Parker, bring in the doctor's bag, will you?'

'Very good, sir.'

Parker went out. As I was about to speak, Ackroyd raised his hand.

'Don't say anything yet. And make certain that window's closed, will you?'

I got up and went to it. It was an ordinary sash window. The heavy blue curtains were closed, but the window itself was open at the top.

Parker re-entered with my bag while I was still at the window.

'That's done,' I said as the door closed behind Parker. 'What's the matter with you, Ackroyd?'

'I'm in mental agony,' he said. 'Yesterday, Mrs Ferrars told me she poisoned her husband! I want your advice – I don't know what to do.'

'Why did Mrs Ferrars tell you this?'

'Three months ago I asked her to marry me. She said yes, but that I couldn't announce it until her year of mourning was over. Yesterday I pointed out that a year and three weeks had now passed since her husband's death. I had noticed that she had been behaving strangely for some days. She – she told me everything. Her hatred of her brutal husband, her growing love for me, and the – the terrible thing she had done. Poison! My goodness! It was murder in cold blood.'

I saw the horror in Ackroyd's face, just as Mrs Ferrars must have seen it.

'But Sheppard, it seems that someone knew about the murder and has been <u>blackmailing</u> her for huge sums of money. The <u>strain</u> of that drove her nearly mad.'

'Who was the man?'

'She wouldn't tell me,' said Ackroyd slowly. 'She didn't actually say that it was a man. But . . .'

'Of course,' I agreed. 'It must have been a man. And you've no suspicion at all?'

'Something she said made me think that the blackmailer might be among my <u>household</u> – but I must have misunderstood her.'

'What did you say to her?' I asked.

'What could I say? By telling me, she made me as guilty as herself, unless I reported her to the police. She made me promise to do nothing for twenty-four hours. I <u>swear</u> to you,

Sheppard, that it never entered my head what she was going to do. Suicide! And I drove her to it – she saw the awful shock on my face, the horror of what she'd done. But what am I to do now? The poor lady is dead. Why bring up past trouble? But how am I to get hold of that <u>scoundrel</u> who blackmailed her to her death?'

'I see,' I said. 'The person ought to be punished, but the cost must be understood – her <u>reputation</u> ruined, suspicion that you really might have been her <u>accomplice</u> . . .'

'Look here, Sheppard, suppose we leave it like this. If no word comes from her after twenty-four hours, we won't say anything.'

'What do you mean by word coming from her?' I asked <u>curiously</u>.

'I have the strongest <u>impression</u> that she left a message for me. And I've got a feeling that, by choosing death, she wanted the whole thing to come out, if only to get revenge on the man who made her <u>desperate</u>.'

The door opened and the butler, Parker, entered carrying some letters on a silver tray.

'The evening post, Sir.' Ackroyd took the letters off the tray, then Parker collected the coffee cups and left quietly.

Ackroyd was staring at a long blue envelope like a man turned to stone.

'*Her writing.* She must have posted it last night, just before – before –'

He tore open the envelope and pulled out a thick letter. Then he looked up sharply. 'You're sure you shut the window?'

'Quite sure.'

'I'm full of nerves,' <u>murmured</u> Ackroyd to himself.

He unfolded the thick sheets of paper, and read in a low voice.

'My very dear Roger, – I killed Ashley and now I must die to pay for that. I saw the horror in your face this afternoon. So I am taking the only road open to me. I leave to you the punishment of the blackmailer who has made my life unbearable. I could not tell you the name this afternoon, but I propose to write it to you now. If you can, my very dear Roger, forgive me . . .'

Ackroyd paused. 'Sheppard, I'm sorry, but I must read this alone,' he said unsteadily. He put the letter in the envelope and laid it on the table. 'Later, when I am alone.'

For some reason I tried to persuade him. 'At least, read the name of the blackmailer,' I said. He refused.

The letter had been brought in at twenty minutes to nine. It was ten minutes to nine when I left him, the letter still unread. I hesitated with my hand on the door handle, looking back and wondering if there was anything I had left undone. I could think of nothing.

As I closed the door behind me I was surprised to see Parker nearby. It occurred to me that he might have been listening at the door.

'Mr Ackroyd does not want to be disturbed,' I said coldly. 'He told me to tell you so.'

★ ★ ★

The village church clock rang nine o'clock as I passed by the gatekeeper's cottage at the end of the drive and ten minutes later I was at home once more. It was a quarter past ten when the telephone rang. I picked it up.

'What?' I said. '*What?* I'll come at once.' I called to Caroline, 'That was Parker telephoning from Fernly. They've just found Roger Ackroyd murdered!'

Chapter 5 Murder

I heard the noise of the door chain at Fernly Park and then Parker stood in the open doorway.

'Where is he?' I demanded. 'Have you telephoned the police?'

'The police, Sir?' Parker stared at me.

'What's the matter with you, Parker? If your master has been murdered . . .'

'The master? Murdered? Impossible, Sir!'

'Didn't you telephone me, not five minutes ago, and tell me that Mr Ackroyd had been found murdered?'

'Me? Oh! No indeed, Sir.'

'I'll give you the exact words I heard. "Is that Dr Sheppard? Parker speaking. Will you please come at once, Sir? Mr Ackroyd has been murdered."'

'A wicked joke to play, Sir,' Parker said in a shocked voice.

'Where is Mr Ackroyd?' I asked.

'Still in the study, Sir. The ladies have gone to bed, and Major Blunt and Mr Raymond are in the billiard room.'

'I think I'll just look in and see him,' I said.

I passed through the door on the right of the main hall, into the small inner hall which led to Ackroyd's study. A small flight of stairs to the left went up to his bedroom. I tapped on the study door. There was no answer and the door was locked.

'Allow me, Sir,' said Parker, who had followed me. He dropped on one knee and looked through the keyhole. 'The key is in the lock, Sir,' he said, rising. 'Mr Ackroyd must have locked himself in and fallen asleep.'

I shook the handle and called out, 'Ackroyd, Ackroyd, it's Sheppard. Let me in.'

And still – silence. I picked up a heavy oak chair and hit the door with it. At the third blow the lock broke. Ackroyd was sitting as I had left him, in the armchair in front of the fire. His head had fallen sideways, and just below the <u>collar</u> of his jacket, was a shining piece of metal.

'<u>Stabbed</u> from behind,' Parker murmured. 'Horrible!' He stretched out a hand towards the handle of the <u>dagger</u>.

'You mustn't touch that,' I said sharply. 'Go and telephone the police. Then tell Mr Raymond and Major Blunt to come to the study.'

'Very good, Sir.'

★ ★ ★

When our local <u>inspector</u>, a man called Davis, and <u>Police Constable</u> Jones arrived, Ackroyd's secretary, Geoffrey Raymond, and Blunt, were in the study with me.

'Good evening, gentlemen,' said Inspector Davis. 'Now then, who found the body?'

I explained the circumstances.

'Did it sound like Parker's voice on the telephone, Doctor?'

'Well – I didn't really notice. I just assumed it was him.'

'How long would you say Mr Ackroyd has been dead, Doctor?'

'Half an hour at least.'

'The door was locked on the inside? What about the window?'

'I closed and <u>bolted</u> it earlier in the evening at Mr Ackroyd's request.'

The inspector walked across and opened the curtains. 'Well, it's open now.'

True, the lower sash was raised as high as it could go. Davis produced a torch and shone it along the <u>windowsill</u> outside.

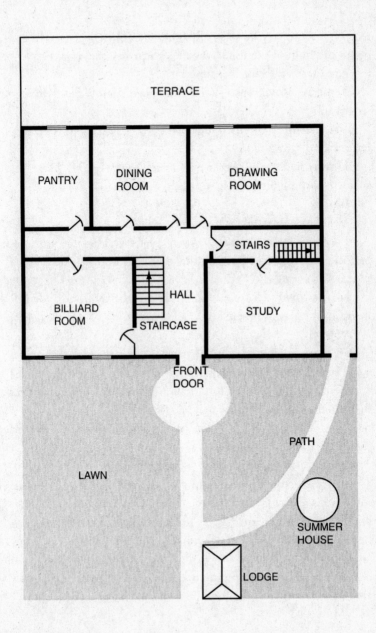

'This is the way he went all right, *and* got in.'

In the light of the torch, several footprints could be seen.

'Are there any valuables missing?'

Geoffrey Raymond, shook his head. 'Not that we can discover.'

I said nothing. But the blue envelope containing Mrs Ferrars' letter had disappeared . . .

'Hmm,' said the inspector. He turned to the butler, 'Have any suspicious strangers been <u>hanging about</u>?'

'No, Sir.'

'When was Mr Ackroyd last seen alive?'

'Probably by me,' I said, 'when I left at about ten minutes to nine. He told me that he didn't wish to be disturbed, and I repeated the order to Parker.'

'Mr Ackroyd was alive at half-past nine,' Raymond added. 'I heard him talking in here.'

'Who to?'

'I assumed that it was Dr Sheppard. I wanted to ask him about some papers I was working on. However, when I heard the voices I remembered he wanted to talk to Dr Sheppard without being disturbed, and I went away again.'

'Who could have been with him at half-past nine?' queried the inspector. 'It wasn't you, Mr – er –'

'Major Blunt,' I said.

'Major Hector Blunt?' asked the inspector, with a respectful tone in his voice. Blunt nodded. 'I didn't see him after dinner.'

The inspector turned once more to Raymond. 'Didn't you hear what Mr Ackroyd was saying, Sir?'

'Only a few words. Mr Ackroyd was saying, "There have been so many demands on my financial resources recently, that I cannot agree to your request . . ." I did not hear any more.'

'A demand for money,' said the inspector thoughtfully, 'and it seems almost certain that Mr Ackroyd himself must have let this stranger in. One thing's clear. Mr Ackroyd was alive and well at nine-thirty. That is the last moment we know he was alive.'

'If you'll excuse me,' Parker said, 'Miss Flora saw him at about a quarter to ten. I was bringing a tray with whisky and soda when Miss Flora, who was just coming out of this room, stopped me and said her uncle didn't want to be disturbed.'

'You'd already been told that Mr Ackroyd didn't want to be disturbed, hadn't you?'

'Yes, Sir. But I always bring the drinks' tray about that time, Sir . . .'

Parker was shaking. His reaction looked more like guilt than shock.

'Hmm,' said the inspector. 'I must see Miss Ackroyd at once. For the moment we'll leave this room as it is. I will just close and lock the window.'

He then led the way into the small hall and we followed him. 'Constable Jones, stay here. Don't let anyone go into that room.'

'If you'll excuse me, Sir,' said Parker. 'If you lock the door into the main hall, nobody can get into this part of the house.'

The inspector then locked the hall door behind him and gave the constable some instructions in a low voice.

'We must get busy on those footprints,' explained the inspector. 'But first of all, Miss Ackroyd. Does she know about the murder yet?'

Raymond shook his head.

'Well, she can answer my questions better without being upset by knowing about the murder. Tell her there's been a burglary, and ask her to come down and answer a few questions.'

In less than five minutes Flora came down the main staircase and the inspector stepped forward.

'Good evening, Miss Ackroyd. We're afraid there's been an attempt at burglary, and we want you to help us. Come into the billiard room and sit down. Now, Miss Ackroyd. Parker here says you came out of your uncle's study at about a quarter to ten. Is that right?'

'Quite right. I had been to say goodnight to him.'

'Was there anyone with your uncle?'

'He was alone.'

'Did you happen to notice whether the window was open or shut?'

Flora shook her head. 'I can't say. The curtains were closed.'

'Do you mind telling us exactly what happened?'

'I went in and said, "Goodnight, Uncle, I'm going to bed now." I kissed him, and he said, "Tell Parker I don't want anything more tonight, and that he's not to disturb me." I met Parker just outside the door and gave him Uncle's message. Can you tell me what has been stolen?'

'We're not quite – certain,' said the inspector.

The girl stood up. 'You're hiding something from me!'

Hector Blunt came between her and the inspector. She half stretched out her hand, and as he took it, she turned to him as though he promised safety.

'It's bad news, Flora,' he said quietly. 'Poor Roger's dead.'

'When?' she whispered.

'Very soon after you left him, I'm afraid,' said Blunt.

Flora gave a little cry, and fainted. Blunt and I carried her upstairs and laid her on her bed. Then I got him to wake Mrs Ackroyd and tell her the news.

Chapter 6 The Tunisian Dagger

I met the inspector coming from the kitchen.

'Do you mind coming into the study with me, Doctor?' Inspector Davis unlocked the hall door and locked it again behind him. 'We don't want anyone to hear us. What's all this about blackmail? Is it Parker's imagination? Or is there something in it?'

'If Parker heard anything about blackmail, he must have been listening outside this door,' I replied.

'That's very likely. I didn't like his manner and when I questioned him again, he told me some story of blackmail.'

I told him the events of the evening.

'Most extraordinary story,' Davis said, when I had finished. 'And you say you couldn't see that letter on the study table when you found Ackroyd? Well, it gives us a <u>motive</u> for the murder.'

'Do you think that Parker himself might be the man we're after?'

'It looks likely. But keep it quiet until we've got all the evidence.'

He crossed over to Ackroyd's body in the armchair. 'The weapon ought to give us a clue.' He pulled the dagger out carefully from Ackroyd and put it in an empty flower vase on the mantelpiece. 'Quite a work of art.'

It was indeed a beautiful object. A narrow <u>blade</u>, and a beautifully decorated handle.

'Take a look at the handle. *Fingerprints!* I want to see if Mr Raymond can tell us anything about this dagger.'

We went back to the billiard room, where the inspector held up the dagger, still in the vase. 'Have you ever seen this before, Mr Raymond?'

'Why – that's the Tunisian dagger. It was given to Mr Ackroyd by Major Blunt.'

'Where was this kept?'

'In the silver table in the drawing-room.'

'What?' I exclaimed. 'When I arrived last night I heard the lid of the table being shut.'

I explained in detail.

'Was the dagger there when you were looking at the table?' the inspector asked.

'I don't remember noticing it.'

'We'd better ask the housekeeper,' remarked the inspector.

A few minutes later Miss Russell entered the room. 'Oh yes, the silver table was open,' she said, when the inspector had put his question. 'I shut the lid as I passed.'

'Can you tell me if this dagger was in its place then?'

'I can't say,' she replied.

'Thank you,' said the inspector.

Miss Russell left the room.

'Let me see,' said the inspector. 'This silver table is in front of one of the French windows and the windows were open. Well, somebody could get that dagger any time he liked. I'll be coming back in the morning with the <u>Chief Constable</u>, Colonel Melrose. Until then, I'll keep the key of that door. I want the chief constable to see everything exactly as it is.'

★ ★ ★

When I got back, Caroline <u>extracted</u> the whole history of the evening from me, though I said nothing of the blackmail.

'The police suspect Parker,' I said.

'Parker!' said my sister. 'That inspector must be a complete <u>fool</u>. Parker indeed!'

With these mysterious words we went up to bed.

Chapter 7 I Learn My Neighbour's Profession

The following morning Flora Ackroyd came to our house.

'Dr Sheppard, I want you to come to The Larches with me.'

'To see that funny little man?' exclaimed Caroline.

'Yes. He is Hercule Poirot, the famous private detective! Uncle promised not to tell anyone, because Monsieur Poirot wanted to live quietly.'

'Flora,' I said seriously, 'I advise you not to involve this detective in the case.'

'I know why you say that,' she cried. 'You're afraid! But Ralph wouldn't murder anyone.'

'No, no,' I exclaimed. 'I never thought he could kill anyone.'

'Then why did you go to the *Three Boars* last night? After Uncle's body was found?'

'How did you know about that?'

'I heard from the servants that Ralph was staying there, so I went this morning. The people there told me that he went out at about nine o'clock yesterday evening and that later you came to see him and went up to his room to see if he was in. This morning they discovered that his bed hadn't been slept in.' Her eyes met mine. 'There *must* be a simple explanation.'

'Well, he wasn't in his room when I got there, so I came home. But I know the police don't suspect Ralph.'

'They *do* suspect him. A man from Cranchester arrived this morning – Inspector Raglan. He had been to the *Three Boars* before me. The barman told me all about the questions he asked. He *must* think Ralph did it. Oh! Dr Sheppard, let us go at once to Monsieur Poirot. He will find out the truth.'

★ ★ ★

'*Monsieur le docteur,*' Monsieur Poirot said. '<u>Mademoiselle</u>.' He bowed to Flora. 'I have heard of the tragedy which has occurred and I offer all my sympathy. In what way can I serve you?'

'Find the murderer,' said Flora.

'I see,' said the little man. 'But if I go into this, *I will go through with it to the end.* You may wish that you had left it to the police.'

'I want the truth,' said Flora, looking him straight in the eyes.

'Then I accept,' said the little man quietly. 'Now, tell me all.'

'Dr Sheppard should tell you,' said Flora. 'He knows more than I do.'

Poirot listened carefully. 'You went to this inn last night? Now why was that?'

I chose my words carefully. 'I thought someone ought to inform the young man of his stepfather's death.'

Poirot nodded and suggested a visit to the local police. He thought it better for Flora to return home, and for me to accompany him.

At the police station we found Inspector Davis, the Chief Constable Colonel Melrose and Inspector Raglan. I introduced Poirot to them and explained the situation.

'The case is clear,' said Raglan. 'No need for <u>amateurs</u>.'

It was Poirot who saved the embarrassing situation.

'I have retired,' he said, 'and I hate publicity. I must ask, that if I help solve the mystery, my name should not be mentioned. If Inspector Raglan permits me to assist him, I will be honoured.'

Raglan was obviously pleased with this.

'Well, well,' said Colonel Melrose, 'we must tell you the latest developments, Monsieur Poirot.'

'I thank you,' said Poirot. 'Dr Sheppard said something about the butler being suspected?'

'Nonsense,' said Raglan. 'These high-class servants get into such a panic with things like this that they act suspiciously for no reason at all.'

'The fingerprints?' I <u>hinted</u>.

'Nothing like Parker's. And yours and Mr Raymond's don't fit either, Doctor.'

We had given our fingerprints to Davis last night.

'What about those of Captain Paton?' asked Poirot.

'We're going to take that young gentleman's fingerprints as soon as we find him.'

'What have you got against him?' I asked.

'He went out just on nine o'clock last night; he was seen near Fernly Park about nine-thirty and he hasn't been seen since. He's believed to be in serious money difficulties. I've got a pair of his shoes here – he had two pairs, almost exactly the same. I'm going up now to compare them with those footprints.'

We all drove up to Fernly in the colonel's car.

'Would you like to go with the inspector, Monsieur Poirot,' asked the Chief Constable, 'or would you prefer to examine the study?'

Poirot chose the study and Melrose took us in. The body had been taken away but otherwise the room was exactly as it had been last night.

'The letter in the blue envelope, Doctor, where was it when you left the room?' Poirot asked.

'Mr Ackroyd had put it down on this little table on his right.'

Poirot nodded. 'Colonel Melrose, would you sit down in this chair a minute? I thank you. Now *Monsieur le docteur*, will you point out the exact position of the dagger?'

I did so, whilst the little man stood in the doorway.

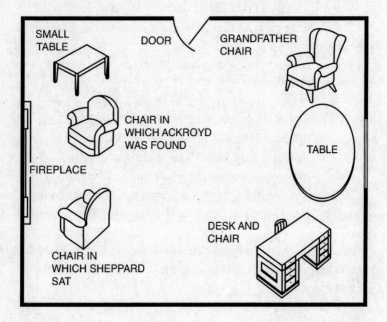

'So the handle of the dagger was clearly visible from the door then?'

'Yes.'

Poirot went to the window. 'The electric light was on, of course, when you discovered the body?'

I agreed, and he came to the middle of the room.

'Are you a man of good observation, Dr Sheppard?'

'I think so.'

'There was a fire burning in the fireplace. When you broke the door down and found Mr Ackroyd dead, how was the fire? Was it low?'

'I – I really can't say.'

The little man shook his head. 'I made a mistake in asking you that question. You could tell me the details of the patient's appearance – nothing there would escape you. If I wanted information about the papers on that desk, Mr Raymond would have noticed anything there was to see. To find out about the fire, I must ask the man whose business it is to <u>observe</u> such things.' He moved swiftly to the wall and rang the servants' bell. After a minute or two, Parker appeared.

'Parker,' said Poirot, 'when you found your master dead, what was the state of the fire?'

'It was almost out.'

'Ah! And is this room exactly as it was then?'

The butler looked round the room 'The curtains were closed, Sir, and the electric light was on. This chair was a little more forward.'

He indicated a high-backed chair to the left of the door, between it and the window.

'Show me,' said Poirot.

The butler pulled the chair out two feet from the wall, turning it so that the seat faced the door.

'Now, who pushed it back into its place again? Did you?'

'No, Sir,' said Parker. 'But it was back in position when I arrived with the police, Sir, I'm sure of that.'

'Raymond or Blunt must have pushed it back,' I suggested. 'Surely it isn't important?'

'It is completely unimportant,' said Poirot. 'That is why it is so interesting.'

'Excuse me a minute,' said Colonel Melrose. He left the room with Parker.

'I wish you'd tell me something of your methods,' I said to Poirot. 'The point about the fire, for instance?'

'Oh! That was simple. You left Mr Ackroyd at ten minutes to nine. The window was closed and bolted and the door unlocked. At a quarter past ten when the body was discovered, the door was locked and the window was open. Who opened it? Clearly only Mr Ackroyd himself could have done so. Either because the room became unbearably hot, but since the fire was nearly out, that cannot be the reason, or because he let someone in that way. And if he did, it must have been someone well known to him, since he had previously been nervous about that same window.'

'It sounds very simple,' I said.

'Everything is simple if you arrange the facts methodically. Ah! Here is the colonel.'

'That telephone call has been <u>traced</u>,' the colonel said. 'It was put through to Dr Sheppard at 10.15 last night from a public call box at King's Abbot railway station. And at 10.23 the night <u>mail train</u> leaves for Liverpool.'

Chapter 8 Inspector Raglan is Confident

'You will be making inquiries at the station?' I asked.

'Naturally, but you know what that station is like,' replied Colonel Melrose.

I did. King's Abbot's station is an important one where different railway lines meet. It has two public telephone boxes. At that time of night, three local trains come in to deliver passengers to the express for Liverpool, which comes in at 10.19 and leaves at 10.23. The chances of someone being noticed telephoning or getting on to the express are very small indeed.

'But why telephone at all?' demanded Melrose. 'There seems no reason.'

'Be sure there was a reason,' Poirot said. 'And when we know that, we will know everything. We should find out if Mr Ackroyd had been visited by any strangers during the past week.'

Colonel Melrose went in search of Raymond, and I rang the bell for Parker. When Geoffrey Raymond came in, he seemed delighted to meet Poirot.

'It will be a great privilege to watch you at work,' he said. Then, 'Hello, what's this?'

Poirot had moved aside and I saw that while my back had been turned, he had pulled out the armchair so that it stood in the position Parker had indicated.

'Monsieur Raymond, this chair was pulled out – like this – last night when Mr Ackroyd was found killed. Someone moved it back into its place. Did you move it back?'

'No. I don't even remember that it was in that position.'

'It is of no importance,' said the detective as Parker came in. 'What I really want to ask you is this: did any stranger come to see Mr Ackroyd during this past week?'

'No,' said Raymond. 'I can't remember anyone. Can you, Parker?'

'There was the young man who came on Wednesday, Sir,' he said. 'From *Curtis and Troute,* I understood he was.'

'Oh! That is not the kind of stranger this gentleman means.' Raymond turned to Poirot. 'Mr Ackroyd had some idea of buying a <u>Dictaphone</u>. The firm sent down their salesman, but Mr Ackroyd did not buy.'

The butler spoke to Raymond. 'Mr Hammond has just arrived, Sir.'

'I'll come at once,' said the young man.

Poirot looked inquiringly at the Chief Constable.

'Mr Hammond is the family lawyer, Monsieur Poirot.'

Poirot nodded. 'Could you please show me the table from which the dagger was taken?'

We went to the drawing room, but on the way Constable Jones <u>waylaid</u> Colonel Melrose, who went with him. I showed Poirot the silver table, and after raising the lid once and letting it fall, he pushed open the window and stepped out onto the terrace. I followed him. Inspector Raglan had just come round the corner of the house.

'Well, Monsieur Poirot, this isn't going to be much of a case. I'm sorry, too, because I like Ralph Paton. A nice young fellow gone wrong.'

'You have worked so quickly,' Poirot observed. 'How exactly did you reach this conclusion, if I may ask?'

'To begin with – method. That's what I always say – method! First, Mr Ackroyd was last seen alive at a quarter to ten by Miss Flora. At half-past ten, the doctor says that Mr Ackroyd had been dead at least half an hour. That gives us exactly a quarter of an hour in which the crime was committed. I made a list of everyone in the house, and worked through it, setting down opposite their names where they were and what they were doing between 9.45 and 10 p.m.'

He handed a sheet of paper to Poirot. I read it over his shoulder.

Major Blunt: in billiard room with Mr Raymond. Major Blunt confirms this.

Mr Raymond: billiard room. See above.

Mrs Ackroyd: 9.45 watching billiard match. Went up to bed 9.55.

Miss Ackroyd: went straight upstairs from her uncle's room. Confirmed by Parker, also <u>housemaid</u>, Elsie Dale.

Servants:

Parker: went straight to butler's <u>pantry</u> – Confirmed by housekeeper, Miss Russell.

Miss Russell: as above, spoke to housemaid, Elsie Dale, upstairs at 9.45.

Ursula Bourne <u>(parlourmaid)</u>: in her own room until 9.55 – then in Servants' Hall.

Mrs Cooper (cook): in Servants' Hall.

Gladys Jones (second housemaid): in Servants' Hall.

Elsie Dale: upstairs in bedroom – seen there by Miss Russell and Miss Flora Ackroyd.

Mary Thripp (kitchen maid): Servants' Hall.

'The cook has been here seven years, the parlourmaid eighteen months, and Parker just over a year. The others are new. Except for Parker, they all seem quite all right.'

'I am quite sure that Parker did not commit the murder,' Poirot said.

'That covers the household,' continued the inspector. 'Now, Mary Black, who lives in the house by the Fernly Park gates – the lodge – was closing the curtains last night when she saw Ralph Paton go past and take the path to the right, which is a quicker way than the drive to get to the terrace. It was exactly twenty-five minutes past nine. He enters the study through the window. At nine-thirty, Mr Geoffrey Raymond hears someone in the study asking for money and Mr Ackroyd refusing. What happens next? Let us suppose Captain Paton leaves the same way – through the window. He walks along the terrace. He comes to the open drawing-room window. Say it's now a quarter to ten. Miss Flora Ackroyd is saying goodnight to her uncle. Major Blunt, Mr Raymond, and Mrs Ackroyd are in the billiard room. The drawing room is empty. He enters quietly, takes the dagger from the silver table, and returns to the study window. He takes off his shoes so that Mr Ackroyd won't hear him, climbs in, and – well, I don't need to go into details. Then he leaves quietly and heads for the station, rings up from there . . .'

'Why?' said Poirot softly. His eyes shone with a strange green light.

'It's difficult to say exactly why he did that,' Raglan said. 'But murderers do funny things. Come along and I'll show you those footprints.'

We followed him to the study window, where the constable produced the shoes taken from the local inn. The inspector laid them over the footprints.

'They aren't the same pair that made these prints. He went away in those. This is a pair just like them, but older – see how the <u>studs</u> are worn down?'

'Surely a great many people wear shoes with rubber studs in them?' asked Poirot.

'That's so. I wouldn't give so much importance to the footprints if it wasn't for everything else. He left no prints on the terrace or on the <u>gravelled</u> path. But just at the end of the path from the drive, look at this.'

A gravelled path joined the terrace a few feet away. In one place the ground was wet and there again were the marks of footsteps, among them the shoes with rubber studs. Poirot followed the path on a little way. 'You noticed the women's footprints?'

The inspector laughed. 'Naturally. But several different women have walked this way – men as well. It's a regular <u>short cut</u> to the house, you see. But it's the footsteps on the windowsill that are really important.'

Poirot nodded.

'It's no good going further,' said the inspector, as we came in view of the drive. 'It's all gravelled again here.'

Again Poirot nodded, but he stayed until the inspector had gone back towards the house. Then he looked at me. 'Luck has sent you to replace my friend Hastings . . . you are always by my side.'

Chapter 9 The Goldfish Pond

'Let us walk a little,' Poirot said. 'The air is pleasant today.'

He led me down a path enclosed by <u>bushes</u>. At the end was a paved area with a seat and a pond of goldfish. Poirot took another path which went up the side of a wooded <u>slope</u>. In one place the trees had been cut down, and a seat looked down on the pond.

'England is very beautiful,' said Poirot. Then he smiled. 'And so are English girls. Hush, my friend, and look at the pretty picture below us.'

Flora was moving along the path we had just left and she was singing quietly to herself. Despite her black mourning dress, there was nothing but joy in her whole attitude. She suddenly turned round, flung her head back and laughed. As she did so a man stepped out from the trees. It was Hector Blunt.

'How you surprised me!' the girl said. 'I didn't see you.'

Blunt stood looking at her for a minute or two in silence.

'What I like about you,' said Flora, 'is your cheerful conversation.'

'I was never good at conversation. Not even when I was young.'

'That was a very long time ago, I suppose,' said Flora.

I caught the laughter in her voice, but I don't think Blunt did.

'Yes,' he said simply, 'it was. It's time I went back to Africa. I'm useless in social <u>gatherings</u>.'

'But you're not going now,' cried Flora. 'No – not while we're in all this trouble. Oh, please! If you go . . .' she turned away.

'You want me to stay?' asked Blunt.

'We all . . .'

'I meant you personally,' said Blunt, with directness.

Flora turned slowly back again and met his eyes. 'I want you to stay,' she said, 'if – if that makes any difference.'

'It makes *all* the difference,' said Blunt.

They sat down on the stone seat by the goldfish pond.

'It's such a lovely morning,' said Flora. 'You know, I can't help feeling happy, in spite of everything. That's awful, I suppose?'

'It's quite natural,' said Blunt. 'You never saw your uncle until two years ago, did you? You can't be expected to <u>grieve</u> very much.'

'You make things seem so simple,' said Flora. 'I'll – I'll tell you why I felt so happy this morning. However heartless you think me. It's because the lawyer has been here – Mr Hammond. He told us about the will. Uncle Roger has left me twenty thousand pounds. Think of it – twenty thousand beautiful pounds.'

Blunt looked surprised. 'Does it mean so much to you?'

'Why, it's everything. Freedom – life – no more pretending to be thankful for all the old clothes rich relations give you. I'm so happy. I'm free. Free to do what I like. Free not to . . . ' She stopped suddenly.

'Not to what?' asked Blunt quickly.

'Nothing important.'

'Miss Ackroyd, can I do anything? About Paton, I mean. I know how anxious you must be.'

'Thank you,' said Flora in a cold voice. 'Ralph will be all right. I've got the most wonderful detective in the world, and he's going to find out all about it.'

Poirot rose to his feet. 'I demand pardon,' he cried. 'I cannot allow Mademoiselle to praise me, and not draw attention to my presence.'

He hurried down the path with me close behind him.

'This is Monsieur Hercule Poirot,' said Flora. 'I expect you've heard of him.'

Poirot bowed.

'I know Major Blunt by reputation,' he said. 'I am glad to meet you, Monsieur. I am in need of some information. When did you last see Monsieur Ackroyd alive?'

'At dinner.'

'And you neither saw nor heard anything of him after that?'

'I didn't see him, but I heard his voice.'

'How was that?'

'I went out on the terrace at about half-past nine. I was walking up and down smoking. I heard Ackroyd speaking to his secretary. I assumed it was Raymond, because Raymond had said just before I came out that he was taking some papers to Ackroyd. I never thought of it being anybody else. Seems I was wrong.'

'Can you remember what the words you heard were?'

'I'm afraid I can't. Something quite ordinary.'

'It is of no importance,' murmured Poirot. 'Did you move a chair back against the wall in the study after the body was discovered?'

'Chair? No.'

Poirot turned to Flora.

'There is one thing I should like to know from you, Mademoiselle. When you were looking at the things in the silver table with Monsieur Blunt before dinner, was the dagger in its place, or was it not?'

'Inspector Raglan asked me that. I'm certain the dagger was *not* there. Raglan thinks it was and that Ralph took it later in the evening. He thinks I'm saying it to protect Ralph.'

'And aren't you?' I asked.

Flora stamped her foot. 'No, Dr Sheppard!'

Poirot tactfully changed the subject of the conversation. 'Look – there is something shiny in this pond. Let us see if I can reach it.'

He knelt down by the pond, pushed up the sleeve of his jacket, and put his arm in the water. However, the mud at the bottom of the pond moved and his hand came out empty.

Blunt looked at his watch. 'Nearly lunchtime,' he said. 'We'd better get back to the house.'

'You will have lunch with us, Monsieur Poirot?' asked Flora. 'I would like you to meet my mother.'

The little man bowed. 'I will be delighted, Mademoiselle.'

'And you will stay, too, won't you, Dr Sheppard?'

We set off towards the house, Flora and Blunt walking ahead. Poirot began to brush drops of water off his sleeve.

'And all for nothing, too,' I said sympathetically. 'I wonder what it was in the pond?'

'My good friend,' he said gently, 'Hercule Poirot does not risk spoiling his clothes without being sure of getting what he is looking for. Before showing my empty hand, I dropped what it contained into my other hand.'

He held out his left hand, palm open. On it lay a woman's wedding ring.

I took it from him.

'Look inside,' commanded Poirot. I did so. Inside was fine writing:

From R., March 13th.

I looked at Poirot, but I saw that he did not wish to say anything more.

Three possibilities came to my mind: the obvious one being that Ralph had secretly married Flora despite her uncle's disapproval at that time. That Roger Ackroyd had been secretly married to Mrs Ferrars – or the least likely, that Roger Ackroyd had married his housekeeper, Miss Russell . . .

Chapter 10 The Parlourmaid

We found Mrs Ackroyd in the hall. With her was a small man with sharp grey eyes.

'Mr Hammond is staying to lunch with us,' said Mrs Ackroyd. 'You know Major Blunt, Mr Hammond? And dear Dr Sheppard – a close friend of poor Roger's. And, let me see . . .'

'This is Monsieur Poirot, Mother. I told you about him. He is going to find out who killed Uncle.'

Poirot went up to the lawyer, and spoke to him quietly. I joined them – then hesitated.

'Perhaps I'm intruding,' I said.

'Not at all,' cried Poirot. 'You and I, *Monsieur le docteur,* we investigate this business side by side. I desire a little information from the good Mr Hammond.'

'I cannot seriously believe that Captain Paton can be involved in this crime,' the lawyer said. 'The fact that he was in need of money is nothing. It was a permanent condition with Ralph. He was always asking his stepfather for money.'

'Mr Hammond, seeing that I am acting for Miss Ackroyd, you will not object to telling me the <u>terms</u> of Mr Ackroyd's will?'

'They are quite simple. After paying certain <u>legacies</u> . . .'

'Such as . . .?' interrupted Poirot.

'A thousand pounds to his housekeeper, Miss Russell; fifty pounds to the cook, Emma Cooper; five hundred pounds to his secretary, Mr Geoffrey Raymond. Then to various hospitals . . .'

Poirot held up his hand. 'Ah! The <u>charitable bequests</u>, they do not interest me.'

'Quite so. The <u>income</u> on ten thousand pounds' worth of <u>shares</u> is to be paid to Mrs Cecil Ackroyd during her lifetime.

Miss Flora Ackroyd inherits twenty thousand pounds. Everything else − including this property, and the shares in Ackroyd and Son − is left to his <u>adopted</u> son, Ralph Paton. Captain Paton will be a very wealthy young man.'

★ ★ ★

After lunch, the lawyer asked Mrs Ackroyd: 'Now, have you all the cash you need for now? If not, I can arrange to let you have whatever you require.'

'That ought to be all right,' said Raymond. 'Mr Ackroyd cashed a <u>cheque</u> for a hundred pounds yesterday. For wages and other expenses due today.'

'Where is this money?' Hammond asked. 'In his desk?'

'No, he always kept his cash in his bedroom.'

'I think,' said the lawyer, 'we ought to make sure the money is there before I leave.'

'Certainly,' agreed the secretary. 'I'll take you up now . . . Oh! I forgot. The door is locked.'

A few minutes later, Inspector Raglan joined us and brought the key with him. He unlocked the door and we went up the small staircase. At the top of the stairs the door into Ackroyd's bedroom stood open. The inspector opened the curtains, letting in the sunlight, and Geoffrey Raymond went to the top drawer of a desk and took out a round leather box. Opening it, he took out a thick wallet.

'Here is the money,' he said, taking out some banknotes. 'You will find the hundred there. Mr Ackroyd put it in the box in my presence last night when he was dressing for dinner.'

Mr Hammond took the notes and counted them. He looked up sharply. 'There are only sixty pounds here.'

'But − I don't understand it,' cried the secretary.

'It is very simple,' remarked Poirot. 'Either Mr Ackroyd paid out that forty pounds some time last evening, or else it has been stolen.'

The inspector turned to Mrs Ackroyd. 'Which of the servants would usually come in here yesterday evening?'

'The housemaid would get the bed ready.'

'I think we ought to clear this matter up,' said the inspector. 'The other servants are all right, as far as you know? Has anything gone missing before?'

'No.'

'Are any of them leaving?'

'The parlourmaid gave notice yesterday, I believe.'

'To you?'

'Oh, no. Miss Russell deals with household matters.'

Poirot and I accompanied the inspector to the housekeeper's room. She said the housemaid, Elsie Dale, had been at Fernly for five months. A nice girl, and most respectable, with good references.

'What about the parlourmaid?' asked Poirot.

'She is clearly better educated than most servants and very quiet and ladylike. An excellent worker.'

'Then why is she leaving?' asked the inspector.

'I understand Mr Ackroyd was very angry at something she had done yesterday afternoon and she gave notice. Perhaps you'd like to see her yourselves?'

Ursula Bourne came as instructed. She was a tall girl, with a lot of brown hair rolled tightly away at the back of her neck, and very steady grey eyes.

'You are Ursula Bourne?' asked the inspector.

'Yes, Sir.'

'I understand you are leaving?'

'Yes, Sir.'

'Why is that?'

'It was my job to tidy the study and I disturbed some papers on Mr Ackroyd's desk. He was very angry about it and I said I had better leave. He told me to go as soon as possible.'

'Were you in Mr Ackroyd's bedroom last night?'

'No, sir. That is Elsie's work. I never went upstairs.'

'I must tell you, my girl, that a large sum of money is missing from Mr Ackroyd's room.'

Her face reddened. 'If you think I took it, and that is why Mr Ackroyd <u>dismissed</u> me, you are wrong. You can search my things if you like.'

'It was yesterday afternoon that Mr Ackroyd dismissed you – or you dismissed yourself, was it not?' Poirot asked.

The girl nodded.

'How long did the discussion last between you and Mr Ackroyd? Twenty minutes? Half an hour?'

'Something like that.'

'Thank you, Mademoiselle.'

I looked at him. His eyes were shining.

Ursula Bourne left and the inspector turned to Miss Russell. 'Have you got her references?'

Miss Russell moved to a desk and took out a handful of letters. She selected one and handed it to the inspector.

'Hmm,' he said. 'It seems to be all right. Her last job was at Marby Grange, Marby – with Mrs Richard Folliott. Well, let's have a look at Elsie Dale.'

Elsie Dale answered our questions easily, and was very upset about the loss of the money.

'I don't think there's anything wrong with her,' observed the inspector, when she had gone. 'Well, thank you very much,

Miss Russell. It's highly probable Mr Ackroyd spent that money himself.'

I left the house with Poirot.

'I wonder,' I said, 'what the papers Ursula Bourne disturbed were? They must have been important for Ackroyd to be so angry.'

'The secretary said there were no papers of particular importance on the desk,' said Poirot quietly. 'So why would he have been so angry with her?'

I had no answer.

Chapter 11 Poirot Pays a Call

On Sunday, after seeing my patients, I arrived home at about six o'clock.

'I've had a very interesting afternoon,' began Caroline.

'Have you?' I said. 'Did Miss Gannett come for tea?'

'No, Monsieur Poirot! Now, what do you think of that?'

I thought a good many things of it, but I was careful not to say them to Caroline.

'What did he talk about?' I asked.

'He told me a lot about himself and his cases. And naturally we talked about the murder. I was able to correct Monsieur Poirot on several points. He was very grateful to me. He said I could make an excellent detective, with a wonderful understanding of human nature. He talked a lot about the <u>little grey cells</u> of the brain. His own, he says, are of the first quality.'

'He isn't <u>modest</u>, is he?'

'He thought that it was very important for Ralph to be found as soon as possible, and explain himself. He says that his disappearance will produce a very bad impression at the <u>inquest</u>. I agreed with him,' said Caroline.

'Caroline,' I said, 'did you tell Monsieur Poirot what you <u>overheard</u> in the woods that day?'

'I did,' said Caroline.

'You realize you're giving Poirot evidence that will prove Ralph is guilty?'

'Not at all,' said Caroline. 'I was surprised *you* hadn't told him.'

'I took very good care not to,' I said. 'I'm fond of that boy.'

'So am I. That's why I say you're talking nonsense. I don't believe Ralph did it, and so the truth can't hurt him. Therefore we ought to give Monsieur Poirot all the help we can.'

'Did Poirot ask you any more questions?' I inquired.

'Only about the patients you had that morning. Your surgery patients. How many and who they were.'

'Were you able to tell him that?'

'Of course!' said my sister. 'I can see the path up to the surgery door perfectly from this window. And I've got an excellent memory, James. Much better than yours.'

'I'm sure you have.'

'There was old Mrs Bennett, and that boy from the farm with the bad foot. Dolly Grice came to have a needle taken out of her finger, and that American steward off the ship. Let me see – that's four. Yes, and old George Evans with his bad stomach. And lastly, Miss Russell.'

Chapter 12 Round the Table

A joint inquest for Mrs Ferrars and Ackroyd was held on Monday. By arrangement with the police, very little information was allowed to come out at the inquest. I gave evidence about the cause of Ackroyd's death and the probable time. The absence of Ralph Paton was commented on by the coroner, but not stressed. Afterwards, Poirot and I had a few words with Inspector Raglan.

'It looks bad, Monsieur Poirot,' he said. 'I'm a local man, and I've seen Captain Paton many times, so I don't want him to be the murderer – but if he's innocent, why doesn't he come forward? We've got evidence against him, but it's just possible that the evidence could be explained away.'

Ralph's description had been given to every port and railway station in England. His apartment in town was watched, and any houses he visited frequently. He had no luggage, and, as far as anyone knew, no money. It seemed impossible that Ralph could avoid detection.

'I can't find anyone who saw him at the station that night,' continued the inspector. 'There's no news from Liverpool either.'

'You think he went to Liverpool?' asked Poirot.

'Well, that telephone message from the station was just three minutes before the Liverpool express train left.'

'Ah yes, the telephone message. My friend,' said Poirot seriously, 'I believe that when we find the explanation of that telephone call we will find the explanation of the murder.'

'I must confess, I think we've got better clues than that, Mr Poirot,' said the inspector. 'The fingerprints on the dagger, for instance.'

Poirot suddenly became very foreign in manner, as he often did when excited over something.

'*Monsieur l'Inspecteur,*' he said, 'those fingerprints – they may lead you nowhere.'

'Mr Poirot, those prints were made by someone who was in the house that night. And I've taken the prints of every member of the household. Everyone. None of them match.'

'You have taken the prints of everyone? Without overlooking anyone? Both alive and dead?'

The inspector looked puzzled.

'You mean . . . ?'

'I am suggesting,' said Poirot, 'that the fingerprints on the dagger handle are those of Mr Ackroyd himself. It is an easy matter to prove. His body is still available.'

'You're surely not suggesting suicide, Mr Poirot?'

'Ah, no! My theory is that the murderer wore gloves or wrapped something round his or her hand. After the blow was struck, the killer picked up the victim's hand and closed it round the dagger handle. He did this to make a confusing case even more confusing.'

Inspector Raglan stared at the little man. 'Well, it's an idea. I'll look into it.'

Poirot watched him go off. Then he turned to me with twinkling eyes. 'And now that we are left on our own, what do you think, my good friend, about a little meeting of the family?'

Half an hour later we were sitting round the table in the dining room at Fernly. The servants were not present, so there were six of us in all. Mrs Ackroyd, Flora, Major Blunt, young Raymond, Poirot and myself.

Poirot rose and bowed. '*Messieurs, Mesdames,* I have called you together for a certain purpose.' He paused. 'To begin with . . . Mademoiselle, you are engaged to Captain Ralph Paton. I beg you, if you know where he is, to persuade him to come forward. Mademoiselle, his position grows daily more dangerous. If he had come forward immediately, he could have explained himself even if the facts look suspicious. But this silence – this disappearance – makes him look guilty. Mademoiselle, persuade him to come forward before it is too late.'

Flora's face had gone very white. 'Too late!' she repeated, very low.

Poirot leant forward.

'See now, Mademoiselle,' he said very gently, 'it is Papa Poirot who asks you this. The old Papa Poirot who has much knowledge and much experience. I would not seek to <u>trap</u> you, Mademoiselle. Will you not trust me – and tell me where Ralph Paton is hiding?'

The girl stood. 'Monsieur Poirot,' she said in a clear voice, 'I swear to you that I have no idea where Ralph is, and that I have neither seen him nor heard from him either on the day of – of the murder, or since.'

She sat down again. Poirot brought his hand down on the table with a sharp sound.

'That is that,' he said. His face hardened. 'Now I ask everyone sitting round this table, Mrs Ackroyd, Major Blunt, Dr Sheppard, Mr Raymond. You are all friends of the missing man. If you know where Ralph Paton is hiding, speak out.'

There was silence.

'*Messieurs et Mesdames*,' said Poirot. 'Understand this, I mean to arrive at the truth. The truth, however ugly in itself, is always strange and beautiful to those who search for it. I tell you, I intend to *know*. And I *will* know – in spite of you all.'

'How do you mean – in spite of us all?' Raymond asked.

'Just that, Monsieur. Every one of you in this room is hiding something from me.' He raised his hand as a faint murmur of protest arose. 'It may be something unimportant that you do not think affects the case, but there it is. *Each one of you has something to hide.* Come now, am I right?'

He looked questioningly at each of us. And every pair of eyes dropped before his. Yes, mine as well.

'I am answered,' said Poirot with a strange laugh. He got up from his seat and went out.

Chapter 13 The Motives

That evening, at Poirot's request, I went over to his house after dinner. He had placed a bottle of whisky on a small table, with water and a glass. He himself was making hot chocolate. He inquired politely about my sister, who he said was a most interesting woman.

'You will have got all the local gossip from her,' I said. 'True, and untrue.'

'And a great deal of valuable information,' he added quietly. 'Women, they are marvellous! They observe a thousand little details, without knowing that they are doing so. Their <u>subconscious</u> mind adds these little things together – and they call the result <u>intuition</u>.'

'I wish you'd tell me', I said, 'what you really think of it all.'

'You have seen what I have seen. Should our ideas not be the same?'

'I'm afraid you're laughing at me. I've no experience of matters of this kind.'

Poirot smiled at me. 'So I give you, then, a little lecture. The first thing is to get a clear history of what happened that evening – always remembering that the person who speaks may be lying. Now first – Dr Sheppard leaves the house at ten minutes to nine. How do I know that?'

'Because I told you so.'

'You might not be speaking the truth. But Parker also says that you left the house at ten minutes to nine. So we accept that and pass on. At nine o'clock you leave the Park gates. How do I know that that is so?'

'I told you so,' I began again, but Poirot interrupted me with a gesture of impatience.

'Ah! You are a little stupid tonight, my friend. *You* know that it is so – but how am *I* to know? You do not use your little grey cells. Now, what did you think of the parlourmaid's story? Does it take half an hour to dismiss a servant? Was the story of those important papers true? Tell me now your own ideas.'

I took a piece of paper from my pocket. 'I wrote down a few suggestions,' I said.

'But excellent – you have method. Let us hear them.'

'To begin with, one must look at the thing logically . . .'

'Just what my poor friend Hastings used to say,' interrupted Poirot, 'but alas, he never did so!'

'*Point No. 1* Mr Ackroyd was heard talking to someone at half-past nine.

'*Point No. 2* At some time during the evening Ralph Paton must have come in through the window – the prints of his shoes tell us that.

'*Point No. 3* Mr Ackroyd would only have let in someone he knew.

'*Point No. 4* The person with Mr Ackroyd at nine-thirty was asking for money. We know Ralph Paton needed money.

'These four points go to show that the person with Mr Ackroyd at nine-thirty was Ralph Paton. But we know that Mr Ackroyd was alive at a quarter to ten, therefore it was not Ralph who killed him. Ralph left the window open. Afterwards the murderer came in that way.'

'Decidedly you have little grey cells of a kind,' said Poirot. 'But what about the telephone call, the pushed-out chair? Then there is the missing forty pounds.'

'Given by Ackroyd to Ralph. He may have reconsidered his first refusal.'

'That still leaves one thing unexplained. Why was Blunt so certain that it was Raymond with Mr Ackroyd at nine-thirty?'

'He explained that,' I said.

'I will not pursue the point. Tell me, instead, what were Ralph Paton's reasons for disappearing?'

'Ackroyd was murdered a few minutes after Ralph left. He must have been afraid he would be accused, and ran away. Men have been known to act guiltily when they're perfectly innocent.'

'Yes, that is true,' said Poirot. 'But we must not forget one thing.'

'I know what you're going to say. Motive. Ralph Paton inherits a great fortune by his stepfather's death.'

'That is one motive,' agreed Poirot. 'But do you realize that there are three separate motives staring us in the face? Somebody stole the blue envelope and its contents. That is one motive. Blackmail! And the blackmailer could have been Ralph Paton. Then there is the fact that he was in some sort of trouble which he feared Ackroyd might discover. And finally there is the one you have just mentioned.'

'Well,' I said, 'the case does seem strong against him.'

'Does it?' said Poirot. 'That is where we disagree, you and I. Three motives – it is almost too much. I am inclined to believe that, after all, Ralph Paton is innocent.'

Chapter 14 Mrs Ackroyd

Mrs Ackroyd asked me to visit her early on Tuesday morning. She was in bed.

'Well, Mrs Ackroyd,' I said, 'what's the matter with you?'

'It's the shock of poor Roger's death. And then yesterday, that meeting with that dreadful little Frenchman – or Belgian – or whatever he is. He was <u>bullying</u> us. Does he really imagine I'm hiding something? He – he – positively *accused* me yesterday.'

'It doesn't matter, surely, Mrs Ackroyd. Since you are not hiding anything . . .'

Mrs Ackroyd looked away. 'Servants do gossip, and talk amongst themselves. And then <u>rumours</u> get round everyone . . . You were with Monsieur Poirot all the time, weren't you, Doctor? It was that girl, Ursula Bourne, wasn't it? She's leaving. *She* would want to make all the trouble she could. You must know exactly what she said. That girl may have said all sorts of things about – about something she saw me do, just to cause trouble.'

Poirot had been right. Of the six people round the table yesterday, Mrs Ackroyd at least had something to hide.

'If I were you, Mrs Ackroyd,' I said, 'I would tell Monsieur Poirot whatever it is you're hiding.'

'Oh!' Mrs Ackroyd began crying. 'I had hoped, Doctor, that you might tell Monsieur Poirot – explain it, you know. Even the smallest bill for something I'd bought – Roger would question it, as if he earned only a few hundred pounds a year instead of being a very wealthy man. Those dreadful bills! Some I didn't like to show Roger at all . . .

'And then I got a letter from a Scottish gentleman – Mr Bruce MacPherson, who was prepared to lend me anything from ten pounds to ten thousand pounds . . . I wrote to him, but there were difficulties. He needed to know that I would be able to repay the loan. And although I expected that Roger would provide for me on his death, I didn't *know*. I thought that if only I could see his will . . . Well, on Friday afternoon everyone was out, or so I thought. And I went into Roger's study – I had a real reason for going there – and when I saw all the papers on the desk, I suddenly had an idea: "I wonder if Roger keeps his will in one of the drawers of the desk."'

'I see,' I said. 'So you searched the desk. Did you find the will?'

Mrs Ackroyd gave a little scream. 'How bad it sounds! But it wasn't at all like that really. In dear Roger's place, I would have said what I was leaving people in my will. But men are so secretive . . . But then, as I was searching, Ursula Bourne came in. It was very awkward. I shut the drawer and stood up, and I called her attention to some dust on the top of the desk. But I didn't like the way she looked – almost disapproving. I have never liked that girl very much. She's too well educated for a servant. You can't tell who are ladies and who aren't these days.'

'And what happened next?'

'Roger came in. He said, "What's all this?" and I said, "Nothing. I just came in to fetch the newspaper." And I took it and went out with it. I heard Bourne asking Roger if she could speak to him for a minute. I went straight up to my room, to lie down. I was very upset.'

There was a pause.

'You *will* explain to Monsieur Poirot, won't you? You can see for yourself what a very small matter the whole thing was. But, of course, when Monsieur Poirot was so <u>strict</u> about hiding things, I thought of this at once.'

'That is all?' I said. 'You have told me everything?'

'Ye-es,' said Mrs Ackroyd.

I noted the hesitation, and I knew that there was still something she was keeping back. It was nothing less than a flash of genius that made me ask my next question.

'Mrs Ackroyd,' I said, 'was it you who left the silver table open?'

'How did you know?' she whispered. 'I – you see – there were one or two pieces of valuable silver. I had been reading about silver and there was a photograph of a small piece that had been sold for a huge amount of money. It looked just like one of the pieces in the silver table. I thought I would take it up to London with me – and – and have it valued. Then, if it really was a valuable piece, just think what a lovely surprise it would have been for Roger.'

'Why did you leave the lid open?' I asked.

'I heard footsteps coming along the terrace. I hurried out of the room and just got up the stairs before Parker opened the front door to you.'

'That must have been Miss Russell,' I said thoughtfully. Mrs Ackroyd had revealed something extremely interesting. Miss Russell must have entered the drawing room by the French window. Where had she been?

★ ★ ★

When I returned home, I discovered that Poirot had visited Caroline.

'I am helping him with the case. Monsieur Poirot wanted me to find out whether Ralph Paton's boots were black or brown.'

I stared at her. I see now that I was unbelievably stupid about these boots.

'They were brown shoes,' I said. 'I saw them.'

'Not shoes, James, *boots*. Monsieur Poirot wanted to know whether a pair of boots Ralph had with him at the hotel were brown or black. A lot depends on this.'

'And how are you going to find out?' I asked.

Caroline said she already had. 'Monsieur Poirot thought they were probably brown. He was wrong. They're black.' Caroline evidently felt that she had scored a point over Poirot.

I did not answer. I was puzzling over what connection the colour of a pair of Ralph Paton's boots had with the case.

Chapter 15 Geoffrey Raymond

That afternoon when I returned from seeing my patients, Caroline told me that Geoffrey Raymond had just left.

'Did he want to see me?' I asked.

'It was Monsieur Poirot he wanted to see,' Caroline said. 'He'd just come from The Larches. Monsieur Poirot was out and Mr Raymond thought that he might be here. He said he would come back and went away. A great pity, because Monsieur Poirot came in almost the minute after he left.'

'Came in here?'

'No, to his own house.'

'How do you know?'

'The side window,' Caroline explained. 'I can see the front door from there. Aren't you going across to The Larches?'

'My dear Caroline,' I said, 'what for?'

'You might hear what it's all about. And you might tell Monsieur Poirot about the boots.'

Poirot got up to meet me, with a look of pleasure, when I arrived at the Larches.

'Sit down, my good friend,' he said. 'You have something for me, yes?'

'Information – of a kind.'

I told him of my interview with Mrs Ackroyd.

'That explains something to me,' he said thoughtfully. 'And it confirms the evidence of the housekeeper. She said, you remember, that she found the lid of the silver table open and closed it as she walked past it.'

'Yes,' I said. 'But why did she come in through the French windows? By the way, I've got a message for you from my sister. Ralph Paton's boots were black, not brown.'

'Ah!' said Poirot sadly. 'That is a pity.'

He gave no explanation about why. Then the door opened and Geoffrey Raymond came in.

'Perhaps I'd better leave,' I suggested.

'Please don't go because of me, Doctor,' said Raymond. 'I just have a <u>confession</u> to make. You accused us all of hiding something, Monsieur Poirot. I <u>plead guilty</u>. I was <u>in debt</u> – badly, and Ackroyd's five hundred pounds will solve all my problems.'

He smiled with that openness that made him such a likeable youngster.

'You are a very wise young man,' said Poirot, nodding with approval. 'You see, when I know someone is hiding things from me, I suspect that the thing hidden may be something very bad indeed. You have done well.'

'I'm glad I'm cleared from suspicion,' laughed Raymond. 'I'll leave now.'

'So that is that,' I remarked, as the door closed behind the young secretary.

'Yes,' agreed Poirot. 'But have you thought, my friend, that many people in that house will benefit by Mr Ackroyd's death? Only one, in fact, does not – Major Blunt.'

The way he said Blunt's name was so strange that I looked up, puzzled.

'You think he has something to <u>conceal</u> also?'

'There is a saying, is there not, that Englishmen conceal only one thing – their love? No, I would like to try a little experiment with Parker.'

'Parker?'

'Yes, Parker. My thoughts always return to Parker – not as the murderer – but perhaps he is the scoundrel who blackmailed Mrs Ferrars?'

'Parker might have taken the letter,' I said. 'It wasn't until later that I noticed it was gone.'

'Then, my friend, will you accompany me to Fernly?'

We set out at once. At Fernly, Poirot asked to see Miss Ackroyd, and she came to us.

'Mademoiselle Flora,' said Poirot, 'I am not yet satisfied of the innocence of Parker. With your help, I want to have him repeat some of his actions on that night. But we must think of something to tell him – ah! I have it. Now, ring the servant's bell for Parker, if you will be so good, Doctor.'

I did so, and the butler soon appeared. 'You rang, Sir?'

'Yes, my good Parker,' said Poirot. 'I have in mind a little experiment. I know that on the night of the murder, Major Blunt was on the terrace outside the study window. I want to see if anyone there could have heard the voices of Miss Ackroyd and yourself in the small hall that night. I want you to repeat that scene. Could you please get the tray you were carrying?'

Parker left, and we went and stood outside the study door. Soon Parker appeared in the doorway, carrying a tray with whisky and water.

'Now, let us do everything just as it happened,' cried Poirot, seeming very excited. 'You came from the outer hall and Mademoiselle was – where?'

'Here,' said Flora, 'I had just closed the door.'

'Yes, Miss,' agreed Parker. 'Your hand was still on the handle as it is now.'

'Then,' said Poirot, 'begin the play.'

Flora stood with her hand on the door handle, and Parker came through the door from the main hall. He stopped just inside the door. Flora spoke.

'Oh! Parker. Mr Ackroyd doesn't want to be disturbed again tonight.'

'Is that right?' she added.

'I think you said "this evening", not "tonight" Miss Flora,' Then, raising his voice in a theatrical fashion, Parker said, 'Very good, Miss. Shall I lock up as usual?'

'Yes, please.'

Parker left through the door, Flora followed him, and started to go up the main staircase.

'Is that enough?' she asked over her shoulder.

'Excellent!' said the little man, rubbing his hands. 'I have discovered what I wanted to know!'

Chapter 16 Parker

The funerals of Mrs Ferrars and Roger Ackroyd took place at eleven o'clock in the morning. Afterwards, Poirot invited me to go back to The Larches with him.

'With your help I will question Parker!' he said. 'We will scare him so much that the truth is certain to come out. I asked him to be at my house at twelve o'clock. He will be there now.'

On arrival at The Larches, Poirot's housekeeper told us that Parker was already there. As we entered the drawing room, the butler stood up respectfully.

'Good afternoon, Parker,' said Poirot pleasantly. 'Please sit down. What I have to say may take some time.'

Parker sat in the chair Poirot had pointed to.

'Now,' said Poirot, smiling. 'Have you often blackmailed people?'

The butler jumped to his feet. 'Sir, I – I've never – never been –'

'Insulted,' suggested Poirot, 'in such a way before. Then why, my excellent Parker, were you so anxious to overhear the conversation between Mr Ackroyd and Dr Sheppard the other evening, after you had heard the word blackmail?'

'I wasn't – I –'

'Who did you work for before Mr Ackroyd?' Poirot demanded suddenly.

'A Major Ellerby, Sir . . .'

'Just so. Major Ellerby was addicted to drugs, was he not? A man was killed and Major Ellerby was partly responsible. It was kept quiet. But you knew about it. How much did Major Ellerby pay you to keep quiet? You see, I have made inquiries,' said Poirot pleasantly. 'You got a large sum of money then as blackmail, and now I want to hear about your latest efforts.'

Parker's face was completely white. 'But I never hurt Mr Ackroyd! Honestly Sir, I didn't. It's true that I tried to listen that night. I heard the word blackmail, Sir, and well, I thought that if Mr Ackroyd was being blackmailed, why shouldn't I have a share?'

A strange expression passed over Poirot's face. He leaned forward. 'Had you any reason to think before that night that Mr Ackroyd was being blackmailed?'

'No Sir. It was a great surprise to me. He was such a gentleman in all his behaviour. I hope you believe me, Sir. I've been afraid all the time the police would discover that business with Major Ellerby and suspect me because of it.'

'I believe that you have told me the truth,' said Poirot. 'If you have not – it will be very bad for you, my friend.'

As soon as he had gone, I asked, 'Do you believe Parker's story?'

'It seems clear that he believes it was Ackroyd who was the victim of blackmail. If so, he knows nothing about Mrs Ferrars being blackmailed because she had poisoned her husband.'

'Then in that case – who –?'

'Precisely! Who? Now we will visit the good Monsieur Hammond.

In the lawyer's office, Poirot came at once to the point. 'Monsieur, you acted, I understand, for Mrs Ferrars of King's Paddock?'

'I did.'

'I thought so. Now, I would like you to listen to the story Dr Sheppard will tell you. My friend, you do not mind repeating the conversation you had with Mr Ackroyd last Friday night, do you?'

'Not at all,' I said.

Hammond listened with close attention. 'Blackmail,' said the lawyer thoughtfully. 'I suspected that might be the case.'

'Monsieur,' said Poirot. 'Could you please give us an idea of the actual money paid to the blackmailer?'

'During the past year, Mrs Ferrars sold shares. The money for them was paid into her account and not re-invested. I once asked her why not, and she said that she had to support several of her husband's poor relations.'

'And the amount?' asked Poirot.

'In all, I should say, twenty thousand pounds.'

'Twenty thousand pounds!' I exclaimed. 'In one year!'

'Mrs Ferrars was a very wealthy woman,' said Poirot. 'And the penalty for murder is death by hanging – and a murderer she was. I thank you, Monsieur Hammond,' said Poirot, standing.

When we were outside, Poirot said, 'We can remove Parker as a suspect. If he had twenty thousand pounds, would he have continued being a butler? No!'

When we arrived at my house, I invited Poirot to come in. We were sitting in front of the fire and smoking, when Caroline entered.

'Have you found Ralph Paton yet?' she asked Poirot.

'Where would I find him, Mademoiselle?'

'I thought, perhaps, you'd found him in Cranchester.'

'In Cranchester? But why in Cranchester?'

I smiled. 'One of the many private detectives who live here – everyone in the village, in fact – saw you in a car on the Cranchester road yesterday,' I explained.

Poirot laughed. 'Ah, that! A simple visit to the dentist. My tooth, it aches.'

Caroline was very disappointed and we began discussing Ralph Paton.

'He has a weak nature,' I insisted. 'But not a <u>savage</u> one.'

'Ah!' said Poirot. 'But weakness, where does it end?'

'Exactly,' said Caroline. 'Look at James here – he would be as weak as water, if I wasn't here to look after him. I've always believed it to be my duty to look after him. If he'd been brought up badly, who knows what <u>mischief</u> he might have got into. Now, as far as I can see, of the people connected to Fernly, only two *could* have had the opportunity of murdering Roger – and that is Ralph Paton and Flora Ackroyd. Parker met her *outside* the door, didn't he? He didn't hear her uncle saying goodnight to her. She could have killed him before she left the room.'

'Caroline!'

'I'm not saying she *did*, James. I'm saying she *could* have done. As a matter of fact, I don't believe she'd kill even an insect. But there it is. Mr Raymond and Major Blunt have <u>alibis</u>. Mrs Ackroyd's got an alibi. Even that Russell woman has one. So who is left? Only Ralph and Flora! And whatever you say, I don't believe Ralph Paton is a murderer.'

When Poirot spoke, it was in a gentle, almost dreamlike voice.

'Let us take a man – a very ordinary man. There is a weakness in him – but it is hidden. Let us suppose that something happens in his life. He is in difficulties – or he may discover a secret by accident. His first thought will be to speak out – to do his duty as an honest citizen. And then the weakness shows. Here is a chance of money – a great amount of money. He has to do nothing for it – just keep quiet. Then the desire for money grows. He must have more – and more! And in his <u>greed</u> he pushes his source of money too far. One can push a man as far as one likes – but with a woman one must not push too far. For a woman has at heart a great desire to speak the truth. How many husbands who have been <u>unfaithful</u> to their wives die and take their secret

with them! How many wives, pushed too far by their husbands'
behaviour, tell their husbands that they have been unfaithful? In
a moment of anger, which they will regret, they tell the truth
with great momentary satisfaction to themselves. So it was, I
think, in this case. The strain was too great. And so, having
confessed to Mr Ackroyd, there was no reason for Mrs Ferrars
to pay the blackmailer more money. But the blackmailer knew
he was about to be revealed. And he is not the same man he was
a year ago. He is desperate. He is prepared to do anything, for if
his crime is discovered, he will be ruined. And so – the dagger
strikes!'

It was as though he had put a spell upon the room. There was
something in the power of Poirot's description which struck fear
into both of us.

'Afterwards,' he went on softly, 'the dagger removed, he will
be himself again, normal, kind . . . But if the need arises again,
then he will kill again.'

Chapter 17 Flora Ackroyd

As I was driving back from visiting my patients the following morning, I met Inspector Raglan.

'Good morning, Dr Sheppard,' said the inspector. 'I'm on my way to the Larches to let Monsieur Poirot know that he was quite right about those fingerprints. They did belong to Mr Ackroyd. However, although he was right about that, I'm afraid to say that in other ways, I don't think Poirot's mind is quite what it used to be . . . That's why he had to retire and come down here. It seems to be a family thing – he's got a nephew who's completely mad.'

'Poirot has?' I said, very surprised.

'Yes. Quietly behaved, I believe, but mad, poor boy.'

'Who told you that?'

A huge smile appeared on Inspector Raglan's face. 'Your sister, Miss Sheppard.'

Really, Caroline is amazing. She never rests until she knows every detail of everybody's family secrets.

'Jump in, Inspector,' I said, opening the door of my car. 'We'll go up to The Larches together, and give our Belgian friend the latest news.'

Poirot received us with his usual smiling politeness. He listened to the information we had brought him, nodding his head. Then he raised a hand.

'But you see, you approach the matter from the wrong base.'

The inspector stared at him, <u>frowning</u>. 'I don't understand what you mean.'

Poirot shook his head. 'Look here; you believe Mr Ackroyd was alive at a quarter to ten.'

'Well, you have to admit that too, don't you, Monsieur Poirot?'

'I admit nothing that is not – *proved*!' Poirot answered with a quick smile.

'Well, we've got Miss Flora Ackroyd's evidence.'

'That she said goodnight to her uncle? But me – I do not always believe what a young lady tells me.'

'But Parker saw her coming out of the door.'

'No. That is just what he did *not* see. Parker saw her *outside* the door, with her hand on the handle. He did not see her come out of the room.'

'But – where else could she have been?'

'Perhaps on the stairs. That is my little idea.'

'But those stairs only lead to Mr Ackroyd's bedroom.'

'Precisely.'

And still the inspector stared. 'You think she'd been up to her uncle's bedroom? Are you suggesting that it was Miss Ackroyd who took that forty pounds?'

'I suggest nothing. But life was not very easy for that mother and daughter. Roger Ackroyd was a strange man over money matters. The girl might be desperate for a little money. Think what happens then. She has taken the money; she goes down the little staircase. When she is halfway down she hears Parker going to the study. If the money is found to be missing, Parker is sure to remember having seen her come down those stairs. She has just time to run quietly down to the study door – with her hand on the handle to show that she has just come out – when Parker appears in the doorway. She says the first thing that comes into her head – she repeats the orders Roger Ackroyd gave earlier in the evening, and then goes to her own room.

'Afterwards it was a little difficult for Mademoiselle Flora. She was told simply that the police had arrived and that there had been a burglary. Naturally she jumped to the conclusion that the <u>theft</u> of the money had been discovered. Her one idea was to stick to her story. When she learned that her uncle was dead, she was <u>panic-stricken</u>. Young women do not faint nowadays, Monsieur, without huge <u>provocation</u>. And a young and pretty girl does not like to admit that she is a thief – especially before those whose good opinion she wants to keep.

'I was always convinced that Mademoiselle Flora was hiding something from us. To satisfy myself, I did the little experiment that I have told you about. Dr Sheppard accompanied me.'

'A test for Parker, you said it was,' I remarked <u>bitterly</u>. Poirot hadn't been honest with me. The inspector stood.

'We must question the young lady right away. Will you come up to Fernly with me, Monsieur Poirot?'

'Certainly. Dr Sheppard will drive us in his car.'

On asking for Miss Ackroyd, we were shown into the billiard room. Flora and Major Hector Blunt were sitting on the long window seat.

'Good morning, Miss Ackroyd,' said the inspector. 'Can we have a word or two alone with you?'

'What is it?' asked Flora nervously. 'Don't go, Major Blunt. He can stay, can't he?' she asked, turning to the inspector.

'If you want him to,' said the inspector. 'But I have some questions to ask you and I'd prefer to do it privately. I think you would prefer it also.'

I saw her face grow paler. Then she turned and spoke to Blunt. 'I want you to stay – please – yes, I mean it. Whatever the inspector has to say to me, I'd rather you heard it.'

Raglan sighed. 'Well, if you really want to. Now, Monsieur Poirot . . .'

Flora looked at Poirot.

'Mademoiselle, what one does not tell Papa Poirot, he finds out. You took the money, did you not?'

There was a silence which lasted for at least a minute. Then Flora sat up straight and spoke.

'Monsieur Poirot is right. I am a thief – yes, a thief. Now you know! I am glad the truth has come out. It's been a nightmare, these last few days! You don't know what my life has been like since my father died and left us with no money. I've bought things I couldn't afford and promised to pay the shops later, knowing I couldn't – oh! I hate myself when I think of it all! That's what brought us together, Ralph and I. We were both weak! I understood him, and I was sorry – because I'm the same. We're weak, miserable things.'

She looked at Blunt. 'But I'm not lying any more. I'm not pretending to be the kind of girl you like, young and innocent and simple. I don't care if you never want to see me again. I hate myself, despise myself – but you've got to believe one thing: if telling the truth would have made things better for Ralph, I would have spoken out. But I knew that it wouldn't be better for Ralph – it makes the case against him stronger than ever. I was not doing him any harm by sticking to my lie.'

'Ralph,' said Blunt. 'I see – always Ralph.'

'You don't understand,' said Flora hopelessly.

She turned to the inspector. 'I was desperate for money. I never saw my uncle that evening after he left the dining room. As for the money, you can do whatever you want. Nothing could be worse than it is now!'

Suddenly she hid her face in her hands, and rushed from the room.

'Well,' said the inspector, 'so that's that.'

Blunt came forward. 'Inspector Raglan,' he said quietly, 'that money was given to me by Mr Ackroyd for a special purpose. Miss Ackroyd never touched it. She is lying with the idea of protecting Captain Paton. I am prepared to swear to it.'

He made an awkward bow, then turning quickly he left the room. Poirot followed him into the hall.

'Monsieur – a moment, I beg of you. I am not deceived by your lie. All the same, what you have done here is very good. You are a man quick to think and to act. The other day I spoke of hidden things. All the time I have seen what you are concealing. Mademoiselle Flora, you love her with all your heart. Oh, why must everyone in England avoid talking about love as though it was some disgraceful secret? You love Mademoiselle Flora. You seek to conceal that fact from everyone. But take the advice of Hercule Poirot – do not conceal it from Mademoiselle herself.'

'What do you mean by that?' Blunt said sharply.

'You think that she loves Ralph Paton – but I, Hercule Poirot, tell you that that is not so. Mademoiselle Flora accepted Captain Paton's offer of marriage to please her uncle, and because she saw in the marriage a way of escape from her life here. She liked him, and there was much sympathy and understanding between them. But love – no! It is not Captain Paton Mademoiselle Flora loves.'

'What do you mean?' asked Blunt.

I saw the dark red blush under his suntanned skin.

'You have been <u>blind</u>, Monsieur. She is loyal, the little one. Ralph Paton is under suspicion, she feels that she must support him.'

'Do you really think . . .' Blunt began, and stopped.

'If you doubt me, ask her yourself, Monsieur. But perhaps you no longer care to – after the theft of the money . . .'

Blunt gave a sound like an angry laugh. 'Do you think I'd turn away from her because of that? Roger was always difficult about money so she got in a mess and was too frightened to tell him. Poor child. Poor lonely child.'

Poirot looked thoughtfully at the side door. 'Mademoiselle Flora went into the garden, I think,' he murmured.

'I've been a complete fool,' said Blunt. 'You're a good man, Monsieur Poirot. Thank you.' He took Poirot's hand and gave it a grip which made Poirot wince in pain. Then he walked quickly to the side door and went out into the garden.

'Not a complete fool,' murmured Poirot, massaging his hand. 'Only one kind – the fool in love.'

Chapter 18 An Untruth

Our drive back to the village was filled with Raglan's complaints. 'All those alibis are useless! We've got to start again and find out what everyone was doing from nine-thirty onwards. Nine-thirty – that's the time we've got to focus on.'

We arrived back at my house and I hurried in to my surgery patients, leaving Poirot to walk to the police station with the inspector.

When I had seen the last patient, I went into the little room at the back of the house. I call this my <u>workshop</u> and I am rather proud of the <u>wireless set</u> I made there. I was just adjusting the inside of an alarm clock when the door opened and my sister Caroline came in.

'Monsieur Poirot wants to see you.'

'Well,' I said, 'bring him in here.'

Caroline returned in a moment or two with Poirot, and then left, shutting the door.

'Aha, my friend,' said Poirot. Coming forward, he sat down and looked at me.

'You know,' I said, throwing down the <u>screwdriver</u> I was holding, 'it's extraordinary. The whole case has changed entirely.'

Poirot smiled. 'Surely it is obvious?' he murmured.

'According to you *everything* is obvious. But it's not obvious to me. It's as if you have left me walking about in a <u>fog</u>.'

Poirot shook his head. 'No, my friend. Take the matter of Mademoiselle Flora. The inspector was surprised – but you were not.'

'I never dreamed of her being the thief! But I've felt that Flora was hiding something – so the truth, when it came, was almost expected. It upset Inspector Raglan very much indeed, poor man.'

'Ah yes! But I made good use of his unhappiness and persuaded him to help me in a small matter.'

Poirot took a sheet of writing paper from his pocket and read aloud. 'The police have, for some days, been searching for Captain Ralph Paton, the stepson of Mr Ackroyd of Fernly Park, whose tragic death occurred last Friday. Captain Paton has been found in Liverpool, where he was about to sail for America.'

Poirot folded up the piece of paper again. 'That, my friend, will be in the newspapers tomorrow morning.'

I stared at him. 'But – but it isn't true! He isn't in Liverpool!'

Poirot smiled with pleasure. 'You have such quick intelligence! I assured Inspector Raglan that very interesting results would follow the appearance of this report in the newspaper, so he agreed.'

'I still do not understand', I said, 'what you expect to get out of this.'

'You should use your little grey cells,' said Poirot seriously. He got to his feet and came across to the bench. 'I see you love machinery, my friend.'

Pleased by his attention, I showed Poirot my home-made wireless and one or two little <u>inventions</u> of my own – small things, but useful in the house.

'Decidedly,' said Poirot, 'you should be an inventor, not a doctor.'

Chapter 19   In The Newspaper

The news about Ralph Paton, invented by Poirot, appeared in the newspaper the next morning and that afternoon Poirot arrived at my house. 'I have something I would like you to do, my friend,' he said. 'Tonight I want to have a little meeting at my house. I need Mrs Ackroyd, Mademoiselle Flora, Major Blunt and Mr Raymond. I would like you to ask them to come at nine o'clock. You will ask them – yes?'

'With pleasure; but why not ask them yourself?'

'Because they will want to know my reasons for having the meeting. And, as you know, my friend, I dislike having to explain my little ideas until the time comes.'

It was then that Caroline opened the door. Her face was full of excitement.

'Ursula Bourne,' she said. 'She's here! I've asked her to wait in the dining room. She's terribly upset, poor thing, and says she must see Monsieur Poirot at once – his housekeeper told her he was here.'

Ursula Bourne was sitting at the table. Her arms were spread out in front of her, and her eyes were red from crying.

'Ursula Bourne,' I murmured. But Poirot went past me with outstretched hands.

'No,' he said, 'that is not quite right, I think. It is not Ursula Bourne, is it, my child – but Ursula Paton? Mrs Ralph Paton.'

Chapter 20 Ursula's Story

Ursula nodded her head once, and burst into tears again. Caroline put her arm around the girl. 'My dear,' she said soothingly, 'it will be all right. Everything will be all right.'

Hidden under her love of gossip there is a lot of kindness in Caroline and soon Ursula sat up and wiped away her tears. 'This is very weak and silly of me,' she said.

'No, no, my child,' said Poirot kindly. 'We all understand the strain of this last week.'

'And then to discover that you knew,' continued Ursula. 'How did you know? Was it Ralph who told you?'

Poirot shook his head.

'You know what brought me to you,' she went on. '*This –*' She held out a newspaper. 'It says that Ralph has been arrested. So everything I've done is useless. I don't have to pretend any longer.'

'Newspaper reports are not always true, Mademoiselle,' murmured Poirot. 'All the same, the truth is what we need now. Now listen, I do truly believe that your husband is innocent – but if I am to save him, I must know all there is to know – even if it does seem to make the case against him stronger than before.'

'How well you understand,' said Ursula.

'So you will tell me the whole story, will you not? From the beginning.'

'What I want to know,' Caroline said, 'is why this child was pretending to be a parlourmaid? Why did you do it? For a joke?'

'To earn money,' said Ursula quietly.

Ursula Bourne, it seemed, was one of a family of seven children, and her parents had lost all their money. Ursula's eldest sister was married to a Captain Folliott. Ursula was determined to earn her living and disliked the idea of being a <u>nursery governess</u> – one of the few professions open to untrained girls. Ursula preferred to get a job as a parlourmaid. It was her sister who had written a reference for her. At Fernly, despite some comment about her obviously good education, she was a success at her job.

'I enjoyed the work,' she explained. 'And I had plenty of time to myself.'

And then came her meeting with Ralph Paton, and the love affair which ended in a secret marriage. Ralph had persuaded her into that. He had said that his stepfather would never let him marry a girl who had no money. Ralph had said that he would find a job and then, when he was earning enough money to support her, they would tell Ackroyd. He hoped however, that this might not be necessary. He hoped that his stepfather might still be persuaded to pay his debts. But when Ackroyd learned how much money Ralph owed, he became extremely angry and refused to help his stepson in any way.

Some months passed, and then Ralph was ordered to come to Fernly. It was now Roger Ackroyd's greatest wish that Ralph should marry Flora, and he told the young man that this was what he wanted. As always, Ralph took the easy way and agreed that he would ask Flora to marry him.

Neither Flora nor Ralph pretended that they loved one another. It was, on both sides, a business arrangement. Roger Ackroyd told them what he wanted and they agreed. Ralph was not the kind of young man who thought about the future, and I believe that he thought the engagement to Flora could be ended after a few months. Both Flora and Ralph got Ackroyd to agree that it should be kept a secret for a month or two. Ralph, of course, was anxious to hide it from Ursula. He felt that her strong and honest nature would not agree to such lies.

Then came the moment when Roger Ackroyd, always determined to be in control, decided to announce the engagement. He said nothing of his intention to Ralph – only to Flora, and Flora didn't object. Ursula was shocked by the news. She wrote to Ralph, demanding that he come down from London to see her. They met in the woods, where some of their conversation was heard by my sister. Ralph implored Ursula to keep silent for a little while longer. But Ursula was determined to tell Mr Ackroyd the truth immediately. Husband and wife parted in anger.

Ursula asked for a meeting with Roger Ackroyd that same afternoon, and told him of the marriage. Their meeting was an angry one – and it might have been even worse if Ackroyd hadn't already been obsessed with his own troubles. It was bad enough, however. Unforgivable things were said by both of them.

That evening Ursula met Ralph by the goldfish pond, going out secretly from the house by the side door in order to do so. Ralph said that Ursula had ruined his life by telling the truth to his stepfather. It was quite possible that Ackroyd would change his will and disinherit Ralph. Ursula, hurt and angry, told Ralph that she hated the way he had behaved.

They parted, still angry with one another, and Ursula, in despair, had thrown her wedding ring into the pond. A little over half an hour later came the discovery of Roger Ackroyd's body. Since that night Ursula had neither seen nor heard from Ralph.

What a damaging series of facts this story was. I knew Ackroyd well enough: he would definitely have changed his will if he had lived. His death came at just the right time for Ralph and Ursula Paton. No wonder the girl had kept silent, and played her part so well.

My thoughts were interrupted by Poirot speaking. '*Mademoiselle*, I must ask you one question, and on it everything may depend: what time was it when you parted from Captain Ralph Paton?'

'It was half-past nine when I went out to meet him. Major Blunt was walking up and down the terrace, so I had to go around the bushes to avoid him. I must have reached Ralph at about twenty-seven minutes to ten. I was with him ten minutes, for it was a quarter to ten when I got back to the house.'

'Mademoiselle, what did you do when you got back to the house?'

'I went up to my room.'

'Is there anyone who can prove that?'

'Prove? That I was in my room? Oh! No. But surely – oh! I see, they might think – they might think –' I saw the horror in her eyes.

Poirot finished the sentence for her. 'That it was *you* who entered by the window and stabbed Mr Ackroyd as he sat in his chair? Yes.'

'Nobody but a fool would think any such thing,' said Caroline angrily. She patted Ursula on the shoulder.

'Horrible,' the girl was murmuring. 'Horrible. I see now. If Ralph heard of his stepfather's murder, he might think that *I* had done it.'

'Now, Mademoiselle,' Poirot said quickly, 'do not worry. Be brave and trust Hercule Poirot.'

Chapter 21 Poirot's Little Reunion

'And now,' said Caroline, getting up from her chair, 'Ursula is coming upstairs to lie down. Don't you worry, my dear. Monsieur Poirot will do everything he can for you – be sure of that.'

'So far, so good,' Poirot said when they had gone. 'Things are becoming clearer.'

'They're looking blacker and blacker against Ralph Paton,' I said.

'Yes, that is so. But it was to be expected, was it not?'

I looked at him, confused by the remark. Suddenly he sighed and shook his head.

'There are moments when I really miss my friend Hastings. Always, when I had a big case, he was by my side. And he helped me – yes, he often helped me. For he had an ability to discover the truth without realizing it. At times he would say something particularly foolish, and yet that foolish remark would reveal the truth to me! And it was his habit to keep a written record of the cases that proved interesting.'

I gave a slightly embarrassed cough. 'As a matter of fact, I've read some of Captain Hasting's work, and I thought, why not try doing something of the same myself?'

Poirot <u>sprang</u> from his chair. I had a moment's terror that he was going to embrace me in the French fashion by kissing me on both cheeks, but thankfully he didn't.

'But this is magnificent – you have written down your thoughts on the case as you went along?'

I nodded.

'Let me see them – this instant,' cried Poirot.

'I hope you won't mind,' I said. 'I may have been a little *personal* now and then.'

'Oh! I understand perfectly; you have written that I am ridiculous now and then? It matters not at all. Hastings, he also was not always polite.'

Hoping that what I had written would be published one day in the future, I had divided the work into chapters. Poirot had therefore twenty chapters to read. Still doubtful, but knowing that I had to go out to a patient some distance away, I gave the pages to him and went out.

It was after eight o'clock when I got back. Caroline brought me a hot dinner on a tray. She told me that she had eaten with Poirot at seven thirty, and that Poirot had then gone to my workshop to finish reading my manuscript.

'I hope, James,' said my sister, 'that you've been careful in what you say about me in it?'

I had not been careful at all, I thought, dismayed.

'Not that it matters very much,' said Caroline, reading the expression on my face correctly. 'Monsieur Poirot will know what to think. He understands me much better than you do.'

I went into the workshop. Poirot was sitting by the window. 'I congratulate you. You have recorded all the facts faithfully and exactly.'

'And has it helped you?'

'Yes. Considerably. Come, we must go and set the stage for my little performance.'

Caroline was in the hall. I think she wanted to be invited to come with us.

'I would have asked you to come if I could, Mademoiselle,' Poirot said regretfully, 'but it would not be wise. You see, all these people tonight are suspects. Among them, I will find the person who killed Mr Ackroyd.'

'You really believe that?' I said, amazed.

'I see that you do not yet appreciate Hercule Poirot for his true worth,' Poirot replied.

At that minute Ursula came down the stairs.

'You are ready, my child?' said Poirot. 'That is good. We will go to my house together. Mademoiselle Caroline, believe me, I will do everything possible to do things as you would wish them to be done. Good evening.'

We left. Caroline, looking as sad as a dog that has been refused a walk, stood on the front door step watching us go.

★ ★ ★

At The Larches, Poirot moved about quickly, rearranging the lighting. The lamps were placed to throw a clear light on the side of the room where Poirot had grouped the chairs, leaving the other end of the room in a dim light. Soon, a bell was heard.

'They are here,' said Poirot. 'Good, all is ready.'

The door opened and the people from Fernly came in. Poirot went forward and welcomed Mrs Ackroyd and Flora. 'It is most good of you to come,' he said. 'And Major Blunt and Mr Raymond.'

The secretary was smiling easily. 'So what's the great idea?' he said, laughing. 'Some scientific machine? Do we have bands round our wrists which register guilty heartbeats?'

'I am old-fashioned. I use the old methods,' admitted Poirot. 'I work only with the little grey cells. Now let us begin – but first I have an announcement to make.'

He took Ursula's hand. 'This lady is Mrs Ralph Paton. She was married to Captain Paton last March.'

A little scream burst from Mrs Ackroyd. 'Ralph! Married! Married to Bourne? Really, Monsieur, I don't believe you.'

Ursula's face reddened and she began to speak, but Flora stopped her. Going quickly to the other girl's side, she put her arm through Ursula's. 'I must apologize for our surprise,' she said. 'We had no idea! You and Ralph have kept your secret very well. But I am very happy about it.'

'You are very kind, Miss Ackroyd,' said Ursula in a low voice. 'Ralph behaved very badly to you.'

'You needn't worry about that,' said Flora. 'Ralph was in trouble and took the only way out. I would probably have done the same in his place. He should have told me the secret, though. I wouldn't have <u>betrayed</u> him.'

Poirot made a sound.

'The meeting's going to begin,' said Flora. 'But just tell me one thing. Where is Ralph? You must know if anyone does.'

'But I don't,' cried Ursula.

'Isn't he <u>detained</u> in Liverpool?' asked Raymond.

'He is not in Liverpool,' said Poirot shortly.

'In fact,' I remarked, 'no one knows where he is.'

'Except Hercule Poirot, eh?' said Raymond.

Poirot replied seriously, 'Me, I know everything. Remember that.'

At a gesture from him, everyone took their seats. As they did so, the door opened once more and two more people came in and sat down near the door. Parker and Miss Russell.

'The number is complete,' said Poirot. There was satisfaction in his voice. 'And every one of you had the opportunity to kill Mr Ackroyd . . .'

With a cry, Mrs Ackroyd sprang up.

'I don't like this,' she cried. 'I would much prefer to go home.'

'You cannot go home, Madame,' said Poirot, 'until you have heard what I have to say.'

He paused a moment, then said, 'Ralph Paton and Ursula Bourne had the strongest motive for wishing Mr Ackroyd dead. But it could not have been Ralph Paton who was with Mr Ackroyd in the study at nine-thirty. Ralph Paton was with his wife. So who was it in the room with Mr Ackroyd at nine-thirty? And now I ask my cleverest question: *Was anyone with him?*'

Raymond did not seem impressed. 'I don't know if you're trying to suggest I'm a liar, Monsieur Poirot, but remember, Major Blunt also heard Mr Ackroyd talking to someone. He was on the terrace outside, and he heard the voices.'

Poirot nodded. 'I have not forgotten. But Major Blunt thought that it was *you* Mr Ackroyd was speaking to and there must have been some reason for him to think so. From the beginning of the case I have been struck by one thing – the words which Mr Raymond overheard. It has been amazing to me that no one has seen anything strange about them.'

He paused a minute, and then quoted softly, '". . . There have been so many demands on my financial resources recently, that I cannot agree to your request . . ." Does nothing strike you as strange about that?'

'I don't think so,' said Raymond. 'He has frequently <u>dictated</u> letters to me, using almost exactly those same words.'

'Exactly,' cried Poirot. 'Would any man use such a phrase in *talking* to another? Now, if he had been dictating a letter –'

'You mean he was reading a letter aloud?' asked Raymond. 'Surely a man wouldn't read letters of that type aloud to himself?'

'You have all forgotten one thing,' said Poirot softly, 'the stranger who called at the house the Wednesday before.'

'The Dictaphone Company,' gasped Raymond. 'A Dictaphone. That's what you think?'

Poirot nodded. 'I contacted the company. Their reply is that Mr Ackroyd *did* purchase a Dictaphone. Why he hid the matter from you, I do not know.'

'He must have intended to surprise me with it,' murmured Raymond. 'He loved to surprise people. He was probably playing with it like a new toy. Yes, it fits in.'

'It explains, too,' said Poirot, 'why Major Blunt thought it was you who was in the study.'

'All the same,' Raymond said, 'this discovery of yours, brilliant though it is, doesn't change anything. Mr Ackroyd was alive at nine-thirty, since he was speaking into the Dictaphone. As to Ralph Paton . . . ?'

He hesitated, glancing at Ursula. 'It isn't that I doubt your story for a moment. I've always been sure Captain Paton was innocent. But he is in a most unfortunate position; if he would come forward . . . '

Poirot interrupted. 'That is your advice, yes? That he should come forward?'

'Certainly. If you know where he is . . .'

'Not very far away,' said Poirot, smiling. 'He is – *there*!'

He pointed dramatically. Everyone's head turned. Ralph Paton was standing in the doorway.

Chapter 22 Ralph Paton's Story

It was a very uncomfortable minute for *me*. I hardly took in what happened next, but when I was sufficiently in control of myself to realize what was going on, Ralph Paton was standing by his wife, smiling across the room at me. Poirot, too, was smiling, and at the same time shaking a finger at me. 'Have I not told you many times that it is useless to conceal things from Hercule Poirot?' he demanded. 'That he always finds these things out?'

He turned to the others. 'One day, you remember, I accused five persons of concealing something from me. Four of them told me their secret. Dr Sheppard did not.'

'I suppose I might as well explain things now,' I said. 'I had been to see Ralph that afternoon. He told me about his marriage, and the trouble he was in. As soon as the murder was discovered, I realized that suspicion would fall on Ralph – or on the girl he loved. That night I told him the facts. The thought of having to give evidence which might <u>incriminate</u> his wife made him decide at all costs to – to –'

I hesitated, and Ralph spoke up. 'To disappear,' he said.

Ursula took her hand from his, and stepped back. 'You thought that, Ralph! You actually thought that I might have killed your stepfather?'

'Let us return to the behaviour of Dr Sheppard,' said Poirot <u>drily</u>. 'Dr Sheppard was successful in hiding Captain Paton from the police.'

'Where?' asked Raymond.

'You should ask yourself the question that I did. If the doctor is concealing the young man, what place would he choose? It must be nearby. I think of a hotel? No. Where, then? Ah! I have it. A <u>nursing home</u>. A home for the mentally ill. So in order to investigate further, I invent a nephew with mental trouble. I ask Mademoiselle Sheppard about suitable homes. She gives me the names of two near Cranchester to which her brother has sent patients. I make inquiries. Yes, at one of them a patient was brought by the doctor early on Saturday morning. Though known by another name, I had no difficulty in identifying that patient as Captain Paton. After certain <u>formalities</u>, I was allowed to bring him with me to my house in the early hours of yesterday morning.'

'Dr Sheppard has been very loyal,' said Ralph. 'He did what he thought was best. I know now that I should have come forward, but in the nursing home, we never saw a newspaper or heard the radio. I knew nothing of what was going on.'

'Well, now we can have your story of what happened that night,' said Raymond impatiently.

'You know it already,' said Ralph. 'I left Fernly at about nine forty-five, and walked up and down the <u>lanes</u>, trying to decide what to do next. I have no alibi, but I promise you that I never went to the study, that I never saw my stepfather alive – or dead. Whatever the world thinks, I'd like all of you to believe me.'

'No alibi makes things very simple, though,' said Poirot, in a cheerful voice. 'Very simple indeed.'

We all stared at him.

'To save Captain Paton the real criminal must confess.' He smiled round at us all. 'See now, I did not invite Inspector Raglan to be present. I did not want to tell him everything I know tonight.'

He leaned forward, and suddenly his voice and his whole personality changed. He suddenly became dangerous. 'I know the murderer of Mr Ackroyd is in this room now. It is to the murderer I speak. *Tomorrow the truth goes to Inspector Raglan.* You understand?'

There was a <u>tense</u> silence. Then Poirot's housekeeper came in with a <u>telegram</u>. Poirot opened it quickly.

Blunt's voice rose. 'The murderer is amongst us, you say? You know – who?'

Poirot had read the message. 'I know – now.'

He tapped the paper.

'What is that?' said Raymond sharply.

'A wireless message – from a ship now on her way to the United States.'

There was complete silence. Poirot stood up and bowed. '*Messieurs et Mesdames*, this meeting of mine is at an end. Remember – *the truth goes to Inspector Raglan in the morning.*'

Chapter 23 The Whole Truth

Poirot made a gesture for me to stay after everyone had left. I was puzzled. There had been a real threat in Poirot's words – but I still believed he had the wrong idea.

He moved over to the fireplace. 'Well, my friend,' he said quietly, 'and what do you think of it all?'

'I don't know what to think. Why not go straight to Inspector Raglan with the truth instead of giving the guilty person this warning?'

Poirot sat down. 'Use your little grey cells,' he said. 'There is always a reason behind my actions.'

I said slowly, 'It seems to me that the first reason was to try and force a confession from the murderer?'

'A clever idea, but not the truth.'

'My second thought is that, perhaps, by making him believe you knew, you might force him out into the open. He might try to silence you as he formerly silenced Mr Ackroyd.'

'And use myself to trap him? *Mon ami*, I am not sufficiently heroic for that.'

'Then surely you are running the risk of letting the murderer escape by warning him?'

Poirot shook his head. 'He cannot escape. There is only one way out – and that way does not lead to freedom.'

'You really believe that one of those people here tonight committed the murder?' I asked.

'Yes, my friend. I will explain exactly how I reached my conclusion. Now, there were two facts and a little discrepancy in time which attracted my attention. The first was the telephone call. If Ralph Paton was indeed the murderer, the telephone call became meaningless and silly. Therefore, I said to myself, Ralph

Paton is not the murderer. I concluded that the telephone call must have been made by an accomplice of the murderer. I was not quite pleased with that deduction, but I let it stand for the minute.

'I next examined the *motive* for the call. That was difficult. I could only get at it by judging its *result*. Which was – that the murder was discovered that night instead of the following morning. But matters were still not clear. What was the advantage of having the crime discovered that night rather than the following morning? The only idea I had was that the murderer, knowing the crime was to be discovered at a certain time, could make sure of being present when the door was broken in – or immediately afterwards.

'And now we come to the second fact – the chair pulled out from the wall. Inspector Raglan dismissed that as of no importance. I, on the contrary, have always regarded it as hugely important. The chair, being pulled out as it was, would stand in a direct line between the door and the window.'

'The window!' I said quickly.

'You, too, have my first idea. I imagined that the chair was pulled out to hide something connected to the window. But I abandoned that thought, for the chair hid very little of the window. But just in front of the window there was a table with books and magazines on it. Now that table *was* completely hidden by the pulled-out chair.

'Now, what if there had been something on that table that was not intended to be seen? Something put there by the murderer? I had no idea of what that something might be. But I knew it was something that the murderer had not been able to take away with him. However, it was vital that it should be removed as soon as possible after the crime had been discovered. And so –

the telephone message, and the opportunity for the murderer to be there when the body was discovered.

'Now, four people were on the scene before the police arrived. Yourself, Parker, Major Blunt, and Mr Raymond. Parker I eliminated at once, since he was the one person certain to be there when the body was discovered. Also, it was he who told me of the pulled-out chair. Raymond and Blunt, however, remained under suspicion. If the crime had been discovered in the early hours of the morning, it was possible that they might have arrived too late to prevent the object on the round table being discovered.

'Now what was that object? You heard what I said in this room not half an hour ago? If a Dictaphone was being used by Mr Ackroyd that night, why was no Dictaphone found?'

'I never thought of that,' I said.

'So, if something was taken from the table, why would not that something be the Dictaphone? But a Dictaphone cannot be hidden in a pocket. There must have been something innocent-looking which could hold it.

'You see where I am arriving? A picture of the murderer is taking shape. A person who was on the scene immediately, but who might not have been if the crime had been discovered the following morning. A person carrying a <u>receptacle</u> into which the Dictaphone might be put . . .'

I interrupted. 'But why remove the Dictaphone? What was the point?'

'Like Mr Raymond you think that what was heard at nine-thirty was Mr Ackroyd's voice speaking into a Dictaphone. But consider this useful invention. You dictate into it, do you not? And at some later time a secretary or a typist turns it on, and the voice speaks again.'

'You mean . . .?' I gasped.

Poirot nodded. 'Yes. *At nine-thirty Mr Ackroyd was already dead.* It was the Dictaphone speaking – not the man.'

'And the murderer switched it on. Then he must have been in the room at that minute?'

'Possibly. But what if a <u>timing device</u> had been attached to the Dictaphone? In that case we must add two more things to our picture of the murderer. It must be someone who knew Mr Ackroyd had bought the Dictaphone, someone with the necessary mechanical knowledge to attach a timer.

'Then we came to the footprints on the windowsill. Here was my conclusion: those prints were made by someone deliberately trying to put suspicion on Ralph Paton. To test this, it was necessary to discover certain facts. One pair of Ralph's shoes had been taken from the *Three Boars* by the police. Neither Ralph nor anyone else could have worn them that evening, since they were downstairs being cleaned. According to the police theory, Ralph was wearing another pair of the same kind, and it was true that he had two pairs. Now, for my theory to be proved correct, the murderer had to wear Ralph's shoes that evening – in which case Ralph must have been wearing a *third* pair of footwear of some kind. It was unlikely that he would have brought three identical pairs of shoes – and the third pair of footwear was more likely to be boots. I got your sister to make inquiries on this point – emphasizing the colour, in order to hide the real reason for my asking.

'You know the result of her investigations. Ralph Paton *had* had a pair of boots with him. The first question I asked him when he came to my house yesterday morning was what he was wearing on his feet on the night of the murder. He replied at once that he had worn *boots* – he was still wearing them, having nothing else to put on.

'So the murderer is someone who had the opportunity to take these shoes of Ralph Paton's from the *Three Boars* that day. And the murderer must have been a person who had the opportunity to take that dagger from the silver table.

'So – a person who was at the *Three Boars* earlier that day, a person who knew Ackroyd well enough to know that he had bought a Dictaphone, a person who was good at mechanical things, who had the opportunity to take the dagger from the silver table before Miss Flora arrived, who had with him a receptacle suitable for hiding the Dictaphone – such as a large black bag – and who was alone in the study after the crime was discovered while Parker was telephoning for the police. In fact – *Dr Sheppard*!'

Chapter 24 And Nothing But The Truth

There was complete silence for a minute and a half. Then I laughed.

'You're mad,' I said.

'No,' said Poirot. 'I am not mad. It was the little discrepancy in time that first brought my attention to you – right at the beginning. You left the house at ten minutes to nine – both by your own statement and that of Parker, and yet it was nine o'clock when you passed through the lodge gates. It was a cold night – not an evening a man would want to walk slowly; why had you taken ten minutes to do a five minutes' walk? All along I realized that we had only your statement that the study window was closed. Ackroyd asked you if you had done so – he never looked to see. Supposing, then, that the study window was open? Supposing, too, that you killed Ackroyd *before* you left? Then you go out of the front door and run round to the summerhouse. You then take Ralph Paton's shoes out of your black bag, put them on, walk through the mud in them, and leave prints on the windowsill when you climb in. You lock the study door on the inside and run back to the summerhouse. Then you change back into your own shoes, and run down to the gate. I did exactly the same things myself the other day – it took ten minutes exactly. Then you went home, which gave you your alibi – since you had timed the Dictaphone for half-past nine.'

'My dear Poirot,' I said, 'what on earth had I to gain by murdering Ackroyd?'

'Safety. It was *you* who was blackmailing Mrs Ferrars. Who knew more about Mr Ferrars' death than his doctor? When you spoke to me that first day in the garden, you mentioned a legacy that you received about a year ago. I have been unable to discover any trace of a legacy. You had to invent some way to explain the twenty thousand pounds you blackmailed out of Mrs Ferrars – money that has not done you much good. You lost most of it in speculation – and then you went back to Mrs Ferrars for more money – and Mrs Ferrars took an unexpected way out of the torture you were putting her through. You knew that if Ackroyd learnt the truth, he would have no mercy on you – you were ruined.'

'And the telephone call?' I asked. 'You have an explanation of that also, I suppose?'

'That was my greatest problem – when I discovered that a call had really been put through to you. At first I believed that you had simply invented the story. It was a very clever idea, that. You needed some excuse for arriving at Fernly and finding the body, and then getting the chance to remove the Dictaphone on which your alibi depended. I had a very vague idea of how it was done when I came to see your sister that first day and asked her which patients you had seen on Friday morning. Among your patients that morning was the steward of an American liner who was leaving for Liverpool by the train that evening. And afterwards he would be on the Atlantic Ocean, well out of the way. I noted that the SS *Orion* had sailed on Saturday, and having discovered the name of the steward, I sent him a wireless message asking a certain question. This is his reply you saw me receive just now.'

He held out the message to me. It ran as follows:

'Quite correct. Dr Sheppard asked me to take a note to a patient's house. I was to ring him up from the station with the reply. Reply was "No answer."'

'It was a clever idea,' said Poirot. 'The call was genuine. But there was only one man's report as to what was actually said – your own!

'Now, remember what I said – the truth goes to Inspector Raglan in the morning. But, because I admire and like your good sister, I am willing to give you the chance of another way out. There might be, for instance, an overdose of a sleeping drug. You understand me? But Captain Ralph Paton must be proved innocent. I suggest that you finish that very interesting manuscript of yours – with the truth.'

'Have you quite finished?'

'There is one more thing. It would be most unwise of you to attempt to silence me as you silenced Monsieur Ackroyd. That kind of business does not succeed against Hercule Poirot, you understand.'

'My dear Poirot,' I said, smiling a little, 'whatever else I may be, I am not a fool.'

I stood. 'Well, well,' I said, with a slight yawn, 'I must be off home. Thank you for a most interesting and instructive evening.'

Poirot also stood and bowed with his usual politeness as I went out of the room.

Chapter 25 Apologia

Five a.m. I am very tired – but I have finished. My hand aches from writing.

What a strange end to my manuscript. I had planned for it to be published some day as the history of one of Poirot's failures! Strange, how things work out.

Poor old Ackroyd. He knew danger was close at hand. And yet he never suspected *me*. The dagger was a last-minute thought. I'd brought a weapon of my own, but when I saw the dagger in the silver table, I thought how much better it would be to use a weapon that wasn't mine.

As soon as I heard of Mrs Ferrars' death, I wondered if she had told Ackroyd everything before she died. When I met him, I thought that perhaps he knew the truth, but that he was going to give me the chance to deny it. So I went home and made my plans. He had given me the Dictaphone two days before to make a small <u>adjustment</u> to it. I did what I needed to, and took it up with me in my bag that evening.

When I looked round Ackroyd's study from the door, I was quite satisfied. Nothing had been left undone. The Dictaphone was on the table by the window, timed to switch on at nine-thirty, and the armchair was pulled out to hide it from the door.

I must admit that it gave me a shock to find Parker just outside the door. Then later, when the body was discovered, and I sent Parker to telephone for the police, I put the Dictaphone into my bag and pushed back the chair to its usual place. I never dreamed that Parker would notice that chair.

I wish I had known earlier that Flora would say her uncle was alive at a quarter to ten. That really puzzled me. But my greatest fear all through has been Caroline. I have suspected she might guess. It was strange the way she spoke that day of my being 'as weak as water'.

Well, she will never know the truth. I can trust Poirot. He and Inspector Raglan will manage it between them. I would not like Caroline to know. She is fond of me, and my death will bring her great sadness. But sadness passes. Discovering that I am a murderer would live with her forever . . .

When I have finished writing, I will put this manuscript in an envelope and address it to Poirot. And then – what will it be? Veronal? That would be a kind of justice. Not that I take any responsibility for Mrs Ferrars' death. It was the direct result of her own murderous actions. I feel no pity for her.

I have no pity for myself either.

So let it be veronal.

But I wish Hercule Poirot had never retired from work and come here to grow vegetable marrows.

CHARACTER LIST

Dr James Sheppard: the local doctor in the village of King's Abbot – he knows everyone in the village and is the narrator of the book

Hercule Poirot: a very famous Belgian detective, now retired – he has lived in England for many years

Caroline Sheppard: the doctor's sister

Roger Ackroyd: an extremely rich businessman who owns Fernly Park, the largest house in the village

Mrs Ferrars: a widow, who owns the second largest house in King's Abbot

Ralph Paton: Ackroyd's stepson

Flora Ackroyd: Roger Ackroyd's niece – the daughter of his dead brother

Mrs Cecil Ackroyd: Flora's mother

Major Blunt: a big game hunter – a friend of Roger Ackroyd

Geoffrey Raymond: Roger Ackroyd's secretary

Miss Russell: Roger Ackroyd's housekeeper

Parker: Roger Ackroyd's butler

Colonel Melrose: the Chief Constable of the area

Inspector Raglan: a senior policeman from the town of Cranchester

Inspector Davis: a local policeman

Constable Jones: a local policeman

Mr Hammond: Roger Ackroyd's lawyer

Ursula Bourne: a parlour maid at Fernly Park

Miss Gannett: an elderly lady who enjoys gossip

CULTURAL NOTES

Mourning

In the 19th century it was expected that a widow would dress in black garments for two years after her husband's death and wear veiled hats. By the 1920s, after the deaths of so many people during the First World War, it was simply expected that widows would wear black and not go into society for a year.

Country house life

The main characters of the book are from the middle and upper classes of society, which in those days had quite distinct levels, based on family money and education.

Rich people often had large houses with farm land in the country as well as sometimes a house in London, and lived comfortable lives with a lot of leisure time. They had a number of servants who lived in these houses, and who looked after the family, did the cleaning, cooking and maintenance.

They often had visitors and guests, who participated in country activities like hunting and fishing. There were also large meals and parties involving considerable expense and luxurious food and drink.

Servants in these houses had their own distinct class system, with different roles for men and women. The butler was the main male servant, and he was in charge of the running of the house. He would greet guests, for example. The housekeeper was the main female servant. She would manage the kitchens, and the work of the maids.

Servants worked long hours for little money, and often worked in the same house all their lives.

People that lived in nearby villages would also supply goods and services to these large houses, and would bring meat, milk, bread and other fresh food to the house every day. In the story, Caroline refers to such people as cooks, maids and gardeners that supply her with information.

Inheritance
This is the money and property left when someone dies. Many people from the upper classes did not have jobs, and lived from investments and inherited wealth. Women in particular were dependent on financial support from their husbands. Marriages were often arranged between sons and daughters of wealthy families, to protect their land and property.

Property and land, on the death of the owner, passed to the eldest son. It is no surprise that Ralph was worried about his future inheritance because, although he was treated like Roger Ackroyd's son, he was not a blood relative.

Money values
Twenty thousand pounds, the amount of money left to Flora Ackroyd in the story, would be worth around £1 million today, using average earnings as the base for calculation. The £500 inherited by Raymond would be about a year's salary for a person in his type of job at the time. The £1000 left to Miss Russell was therefore a very large amount of money for a servant.

The Season
It was customary for upper class and aristocratic families to participate in social events – usually dances – where their daughters could meet suitable men as prospective husbands. The young women were called 'debutante' – from the French word meaning 'beginners'. This process

was called 'coming out' – i.e. the first time a young woman was presented to society. Flora's mother refers to this in the story.

Village life

An English village is a small group of houses in the countryside, usually with a church at its centre. Sometimes there is a very large house in a village where rich people live who may own the local farm land and the houses of farm workers. A village often has a post office, an inn (or pub), and a shop. It may also have a local doctor.

Village life is usually quieter and slower than life in a town and everyone knows who everyone else is, even if they do not meet socially. They also often know quite a lot about each other's lives. Sometimes this means that they help others who are ill or who have troubles. Sometimes this just means that they talk, or gossip, amongst themselves about other people. Caroline, Dr Sheppard's sister, is the centre of village gossip and often misinterprets what she sees and hears, and spreads rumours.

Structure of the police

The structure of the police force and the ranks of the men and women who work there have not changed much since the Metropolitan Police was created in London in 1829. The ranks, starting at the lowest, are: Police Constable, Sergeant, Inspector, Chief Inspector, Superintendent and Chief Superintendent.

Throughout the country there is a structure of separate but co-operating police forces. Each one has a Chief Constable in charge. The Chief Constable does not usually participate in police operations but is more of a manager who makes important decisions. In this story, however, the Chief Constable, Colonel Melrose, becomes involved in the case, as Ackroyd was a very important member of the local community. Inspector Davies and Inspector Raglan are mid-ranking, and would be the typical level of police officer to investigate a murder.

Liverpool
Liverpool, 283 kilometres from London, on the west coast of England, was a major passenger and freight port. In the story, Liverpool is the obvious place for someone wishing to escape the country to get to.

GLOSSARY

Key

n = noun
v = verb
phr v = phrasal verb
adj = adjective
adv = adverb
excl = exclamation
exp = expression

accomplice (n)
someone who helps another person to commit a crime

adjustment (n)
a small change to something to make it more effective

adopted (adj)
someone who has been legally taken in as a child by another family

alcoholic (n)
someone who cannot stop drinking large amounts of alcohol, even if it
makes them ill

alibi (n)
something that proves you were in a different place when a crime
happened; a reason why you can't be guilty of a crime

amateur (n)
someone who does something as a hobby and not as a job; not an
expert

astonished (adj)
very surprised about something

betray (v)
to do something which hurts or disappoints a person who loves and trusts you

billiard room (n)
a room where billiards is played: a game on a large table in which you use a long stick called a cue to hit small heavy balls into pockets around the sides of the table

bitterly (adj)
in a very angry or disappointed way

blackmail (v)
to threaten to hurt someone or reveal a secret about them unless they do something for you or give you money

blade (n)
the edge of a knife which is used for cutting

blind (adj)
if you describe someone's beliefs or actions as blind, you think that they do not question or think about what they are doing

bolt (v)
to lock a door or window by sliding a bolt – a long metal object – across it to fasten it

bully (v)
to use strength or power to hurt or frighten another person

burglary (n)
the act of entering a building by force and stealing things

bush (n)
a large plant which is smaller than a tree and has a lot of branches

butler (n)
the most important male servant in a wealthy house

charitable bequest (n)
to give money to an organization or activity which helps and supports other people who are ill, disabled or poor

cheque (n)
a printed form on which you write an amount of money and who it is to be paid to

Chief Constable (n)
the officer in charge of the police force in a particular county or area

collar (n)
the part of a shirt or coat which fits round the neck and is usually folded over

come forward (v)
to give information in response to a request for help

conceal (v)
to cover or hide something carefully

confess (v)
to admit that you did something wrong

confession (n)
the act of admitting that you have done something you are ashamed of or embarrassed about

cook (n)
a person whose job is to cook and prepare food

curiously (adj)
in a way which shows you are interested in something and want to find out more about it

dagger (n)
a weapon like a knife with two sharp edges

desperate (adj)
the feeling you have when you are in such a bad situation that you will try anything to change it

despise (v)
to dislike someone and have a very low opinion of them

detain (v)
to keep a person in a place under the control of someone else, usually the police

devoted (adj)
to care about someone and love them very much

Dictaphone (n)
a small machine used to record someone speaking, so that their words can be played back later

dictate (v)
to tell someone what they should or can do; to speak or read aloud for someone else to write down what you are saying

discrepancy (n)
a noticeable difference between two things which ought to be the same

disinherit (v)
to arrange that someone, usually your son or daughter, will not become the owner of your money or property after you die

dismayed (adj)
having a strong feeling of worry, fear or sadness

dismiss (v)
tell an employee that they are no longer needed to do the job they have been doing

drawing room (n)
a formal term for a large room in a wealthy or important house, where people sit and relax

drily (adj)
in a way which is clever and funny without being too obvious

drug addict (n)
a person who uses or is addicted to illegal drugs

engaged (adj)
when you agree to marry another person

extract (v)
to get information from a person, usually when they don't want to give it

extravagant (adj)
someone who spends more money than they can afford, or uses more of something than is reasonable

faint (v)
lose consciousness for a short time

Fate (n)
a power that some people believe controls and decides everything that happens

fireplace (n)
a place in a room where a fire can be lit, the area on the wall and floor surrounding this

fog (n)
a cloud or mist; can be used to mean that it is hard to see or understand something

fond (adj)
if you are fond of someone, you like them and feel affection for them

fool (n)
someone who is **foolish**

foolish (adj)
if you say that someone's behaviour is foolish, you mean that it is not sensible and shows a lack of good judgement

formality (n)
something that must be done as part of another activity or event, e.g. paperwork

French windows (n)
a pair of glass doors which you go through into a garden or onto a balcony

frown (v)
to have an expression on your face which shows anger, worry or concentration

gathering (n)
a group of people meeting together

genius (n)
a great ability, skill or intelligence

gesture (n)
a movement you make with a part of your body, especially your hands, to express emotion or information

give notice (v)
to tell your employer that you are going to leave your job

gossip (n)
informal conversation or information about other people's private affairs

gravelled (adj)
having a surface on a path or road of very small stones

greed (n)
the desire to have more of something than is necessary or fair

grieve (v)
to feel very sad about someone's death

hang about (v)
to stay in the same place doing nothing, usually because you are waiting for something or someone

haunted (adj)
very worried or troubled, usually about something you have done

heroic (adj)
brave and determined

hint (v)
to make a suggestion about something in an indirect way

household (n)
all the people who live and work in a house

housemaid (n)
a female servant who does cleaning and other work in someone's house

implore (v)
to beg someone to do something; to ask desperately

impression (n)
what you think about a person or situation, usually after seeing or hearing something them

income (n)
money that you earn or receive

incriminate (v)
to suggest that someone is the person responsible for something bad, especially a crime

in debt (phr)
if you are 'in debt' you owe someone money

inherit (v)
to receive money or property from someone after they die

inquest (n)
an official inquiry into the cause of someone's death

inspector (n)
a police officer of important position

intuition (n)
an unexplained feeling that something is true, without any evidence to prove it

invention (n)
a machine, device or system that has been invented by someone

lane (n)
a small road or path in the countryside

legacy (n)
money or property which someone leaves to you in their will when they die

lid (n)
the top of a container which you lift or open to look inside

little grey cells (n)
an expression of Poirot's to mean his brain

logically (adv)
in a way which uses logic or reason

Mademoiselle (n)
a French title that refers to a young, unmarried woman

mail train (n)
a train which carries letters and parcels

manuscript (n)
a handwritten or typed document, usually the first draft of a book

mean (adj)
not wanting to spend much money

Messieurs, Mesdames (n)
a French term for addressing a group of men or a group of older, married women

milkman (n)
a person whose job is to deliver milk to peoples' houses

mischief (n)
behaviour that causes trouble for other people

modest (adj)
not talking too much about your own abilities, intelligence or skills

Monsieur (n)
a French title that refers to a man

motive (n)
your reason for doing something; a reason for committing a crime

mourning (n)
a time when you show your sadness about the death of another person

murmur (v)
to say something quietly

nursery governess (n)
a woman who works in a large house, looking after the children and giving them an education

nursing home (n)
an institution where people who need medical care, especially old people, are looked after

oak (adj)
the strong, hard wood of a large tree

observe (v)
to watch or study someone or something carefully

obsessed (adj)
thinking about one thing so much that you can't think about anything else

overhear (v)
to hear other people talking when they are not talking to you

panic-stricken (adj)
so anxious or afraid that you act without thinking carefully

pantry (n)
a small room or large cupboard where food is kept

parlourmaid (n)
a female servant in a big house who was employed to serve food at the dinner table

pearl (n)
a hard, round object which is white or cream; it grows inside the shell of an oyster

penalty (n)
a punishment for a crime

plead guilty (v)
to admit in court that you have committed a crime

Police Constable (n)
the police are the organization responsible for making sure people don't break the law; a constable has a low or junior rank within this

privilege (n)
a situation which you appreciate and respect

provocation (n)
a reason for someone to behave unreasonably, angrily or violently

receptacle (n)
an object which you use to put or keep things in

reference (n)
a letter written by someone who knows you well, usually in order to help you get a job

retired (adj)
being an older person who has left their job and stopped working

reveal (v)
to make other people aware of something

ridiculous (adj)
foolish or silly in a funny way

round (n)
a series of visits a doctor makes to his patients

rumour (n)
a story or piece of information that may or may not be true

sash window (n)
a window that consists of two separate parts, one above the other, that you open by sliding one of the parts up or down

savage (adj)
cruel, violent and uncontrolled

scoundrel (n)
a person who behaves very badly towards other people

screwdriver (n)
a tool that is used for turning screws

self-indulgent (adj)
allowing yourself to have a lot of something you like, even if it isn't good for you

share (n)
a part of a company that you buy as an investment

short cut (n)
a quicker way of getting somewhere than the usual route

sigh (n)
a short release of a deep breath, as a way of expressing feelings such as disappointment, tiredness or sadness

slope (n)
the side of a hill

source (n)
the person or place from which you get something

speculate (v)
to buy property or shares with the hope of making more money by selling them at a higher price

spell (n)
a situation in which events are controlled by a magical power

spoil (v)
damage something, to make it less pleasant or satisfactory

spring (v)
to jump up quickly

stab (v)
to push a knife or sharp object into someone's body

stepson (n)
the son of someone's husband or wife, born during a previous relationship

steward (n)
a man who works on a ship, plane or train, looking after passengers and serving meals to them

strain (n)
worry or concern caused by a difficult situation

strict (adj)
being very clear about something and wanting to be obeyed

stud (n)
a small piece of rubber or metal attached to the bottom part of a shoe

subconscious (n)
the part of your mind that can influence your behaviour even if you aren't aware of it

surgery (n)
the period of time in a day when a doctor sees patients

swear (v)
to promise that something is true

telegram (n)
a message that is sent by telegraph (a system of sending messages over long distances) and then printed and delivered to someone's home or office

tense (adj)
being awkward or uncomfortable

terms (n)
the conditions or details of a legal agreement

theft (n)
the crime of stealing

timing device (n)
an invention which can make a machine start or stop at a particular time

trace (v)
to find the origin of where something came from or started

trap (v)
to catch someone; to trick them into doing or saying something

twinkle (v)
to show amusement in your eyes

unfaithful (adj)
to have a relationship with someone else when you already have a partner

value (v)
to have an item examined by an expert to find out how much money it is worth

vegetable marrow (n)
a type of long, green vegetable which is white inside, which is eaten cooked

veronal (n)
a dangerous drug used to help a person sleep; taking too much can kill you

waylay (v)
to stop someone when they are going somewhere, to talk about something

weed (n)
a wild plant that grows in a garden where it should not be

widow (n)
a woman whose husband has died and who has not married again

will (n)
a legal document in which you say what you want to happen to your money and possessions after you die

wince (v)
to show an expression of pain on your face

windowsill (n)
a ledge or shelf along the bottom of a window

wireless set (n)
an old-fashioned term for a radio

woods (n)
a large area of trees growing near each other

workshop (n)
a room or building which contains tools for making or repairing things

yawn (n)
the action of opening your mouth wide and breathing in a lot of air when you are tired

The Mysterious Affair at Styles

Recently, there have been some strange things happening at Styles, a large country house in Essex. Evelyn Howard, a loyal friend to the family for years, leaves the house after an argument with Mrs Inglethorp. Mrs Inglethorp then suddenly falls ill and dies. Has she been poisoned? It is up to the famous Belgian detective, Hercule Poirot, to find out what happened.

The Man in the Brown Suit

Pretty, young Anne Beddingfeld comes to London looking for adventure. But adventure finds her when she sees a man fall off an Underground platform and die on the rails. The police think the death was an accident. But who was the man in the brown suit who examined the body before running away? Anne has only one clue, but she is determined to find the mysterious killer. Anne's adventure takes her on a cruise ship all the way to Cape Town and on into Africa…

The Murder at the Vicarage

When Colonel Protheroe is found murdered in the vicar's study, it seems that almost everyone in the village of St Mary Mead had a reason to kill him. This is the first case for Agatha Christie's famous female detective, Miss Marple. She needs to use all her powers of observation and deduction to solve the mystery.

Peril at End House

The famous detective Hercule Poirot is on holiday in the south of England when he meets a young woman called Nick Buckley. Nick has had a lot of mysterious 'accidents'. First, her car brakes failed. Then, a large rock just missed her when she was walking, and later, a painting almost fell on her while she was asleep. Finally, Poirot finds a bullet hole in her hat! Nick is in danger and needs Poirot's help. Can he find the guilty person before Nick is harmed?

Why Didn't They Ask Evans?

Bobby Jones is playing golf . . . terribly. As his ball disappears over the edge of a cliff, he hears a cry. The ball is lost, but on the rocks below he finds a dying man. With his final breath the man opens his eyes and says, 'Why didn't they ask Evans?' Bobby and his adventure-seeking friend Lady Frances, set out to solve the mystery of the dying man's last words, but put their own lives in terrible danger . . .

Death in the Clouds

Hercule Poirot is travelling from France to England by plane. During the journey a passenger is murdered. Someone on the flight is guilty of the crime – but who could have a reason to kill an elderly lady? And how is it possible that no one saw it happen?

Appointment with Death

Mrs Boynton, cruel and hated by her family, is found dead while on holiday in the ancient city of Petra in Jordan. Was it just a weak heart and too much sun that killed her, or was she murdered? By chance, the great detective Hercule Poirot is visiting the country. He has 24 hours to solve the case.

N or M?

It is World War II and a British secret agent has been murdered. The murderers are Nazi agents living somewhere in England. They are known only as N and M, and could be anyone. The only clue as to where they are hiding points to the seaside village of Leahampton and its busy guesthouse, *Sans Souci*. Tommy and Tuppence Beresford, Britain's most unlikely spies, accept the mission to find N and M. No one can be trusted . . .

The Moving Finger

Lymstock is a small town with many secrets. Recently several people in the town have received unpleasant anonymous letters. When Mrs Symmington dies in mysterious circumstances after receiving a letter, the people of the town no longer know who they can trust. Who is writing the letters? And why? Miss Marple helps solve the mystery.

THE AGATHA CHRISTIE SERIES

The Mysterious Affair at Styles
The Man in the Brown Suit
The Murder of Roger Ackroyd
The Murder at the Vicarage
Peril at End House
Why Didn't They Ask Evans?
Death in the Clouds
Appointment with Death
N or M?
The Moving Finger
Sparkling Cyanide
Crooked House
They Came to Baghdad
They Do It With Mirrors
A Pocket Full of Rye
After the Funeral
Destination Unknown
Hickory Dickory Dock
4.50 From Paddington
Cat Among the Pigeons

Visit **www.collinselt.com/agathachristie** for language
activities and teacher's notes based on this story.